"LOUISE?" JAMIE WAS PERPLEXED. "YOU CALLED her a colleague—but she signed her letter to me 'Aunt Louise.'"

"Your aunt—hmmm." His father looked briefly thoughtful, then smiled again. "Yes, yes, I hadn't thought of it before, but that's exactly what she is."

Jamie was trying to decide how to answer this confusing comment when a sudden wind rammed the rain against the glass.

"Ahh," said his father. "That will be her now. Will you go and get the door?"

Jamie walked to the front hall. He knew that he hadn't heard anybody knock.

BLUE
WOLF

❦

Catherine Creedon

The Julie Andrews Collection

📚 HarperTrophy®
An Imprint of HarperCollinsPublishers

For my mother,
and Ben and Per and Scott,
with love

Epigraph from *Of Wolves and Men* reprinted by permission of Sterling
Lord Literistic, Inc. Copyright © 1988 by Barry Lopez.

Harper Trophy® is a registered trademark of
HarperCollins Publishers Inc.

Library of Congress Cataloging-in-Publication Data
Creedon, Catherine E.
    Blue wolf / Catherine Creedon.— 1st ed.
        p.   cm.
    "The Julie Andrews collection."
    Summary: Following the death of his mother, fourteen-year-old Jamie
is sent to live with his mysterious aunt in the wilds of the Pacific
Northwest, where he discovers some long-hidden family secrets.
    ISBN 0-06-050868-X — ISBN 0-06-050869-8 (lib. bdg.)
    ISBN 0-06-050870-1 (pbk.)
    [1. Wolves—Fiction. 2. Supernatural—Fiction. 3. Aunts—Fiction.
4. Northwest, Pacific—Fiction.] I. Title.
PZ7.C8618 Bl 2003   2002152280
[Fic]—dc21   CIP
                                                              AC

Typography by Karin Paprocki
❖
First Harper Trophy edition, 2005

Visit us on the World Wide Web!
www.harperchildrens.com

The tolerance for mystery invigorates the imagination; and it is the imagination that gives shape to the universe. The appreciation of the separate realities enjoyed by other organisms is not only no threat to our own reality, but the root of a fundamental joy.

—❦ Barry Lopez, *Of Wolves and Men*

Arnica

CHAPTER I

Dear Jamie,

*Your father writes that you are, as
always, perfect. He also tells me that the
exact nature of your perfection has
recently escaped him. Perhaps you should
come for a visit? I would enjoy your
company, and it would give him a much-
needed opportunity to miss you. The choice
is yours.*

Love,
Aunt Louise

"What are you reading?" barked Madame Mahoney.

"Nothing." Fourteen-year-old Jamie Park slid the letter under his French textbook. His teacher narrowed her eyes at him but turned back to the chalkboard. He peeked at the letter, then traced the odd, spidery writing with his finger. As far as he knew, he didn't have an aunt—let alone an Aunt Louise.

Jamie pushed his thick black hair behind his ears and tried to pay attention. Usually he enjoyed French. His mother, a linguist, had shared with him a love of words and stories. His father spoke to him, if he spoke at all, in two different languages: English and Korean. (Three if you counted all the technical terms connected with his research in paleozoology.) And the many scholars and scientists who passed through their home spoke such a variety of tongues that it often sounded to Jamie as if large flocks of birds were seated around the dining-room table. But today his mind wandered. He bent his head and sniffed the letter. Wood smoke, he thought, wood smoke and wet animals. Dogs? Not exactly. He sniffed again, ignoring the stares of his classmates. Wolves. It smelled like the wolves.

"Jamie," snapped Madame Mahoney as the bell rang, "you will stay after class."

"I have a track meet." He had to go. The wolves might be there today.

Madame Mahoney tapped a pencil, eraser end down, on her desk. Jamie knew she was trying to decide what to say to him. Though older and stricter than most of his teachers, she was his favorite. Her hair was dyed flaming red, and when she smiled he could imagine the girl she'd been in Paris before marrying an American and coming to the United States.

Why was she so comfortable here, when his own father, born in Korea, still had trouble fitting in? His dad had lived in Seattle for years but seldom looked beyond the activities of his lab at the university. He'd never even been to one of Jamie's races. Jamie sighed at the thought of his father. Madame Mahoney cleared her throat. Jamie snapped back to attention.

"Jamie," she said, then shook her head. "Here." She handed him a piece of paper. "This is tonight's homework. I noticed that you didn't copy it down. Find me tomorrow at lunch if you need help."

Jamie waited for her to continue, but she flipped the pencil over, bent her head to the desk, and began to correct papers.

Lecture over, thought Jamie. Both relieved and embarrassed, he wondered when the teachers would stop being so nice to him. He hoped it would be soon. Their tolerance, combined with the silence of his classmates, made him feel as though he didn't exist—as though he had died along with his mother. He shoved the assignment and the letter into his pocket, then headed for the locker room.

Jamie jumped up and down, shaking his arms, trying to stay warm. It was the beginning of June, but the rain made it feel more like March. He jogged toward his teammates. They

stopped talking as he approached; some shuffled uncomfortably, others just looked away. Jamie pretended not to notice
and began to stretch. He was the fastest distance runner in
the school; no one could pass him in the fall cross-country
meets. He had to work a little harder at the shorter distances
in spring track, but today was the last race of the season, and
he was determined to win his event.

It was nearly time for the start. He stood with the other
runners, flexing his knees a bit, when he heard it. A panting
sound, faint at first, but steady. It was the wolves—they
always ran with Jamie when he needed them. When he'd first
heard them, at a cross-country meet last fall, he'd been terri-
fied. The wolves had followed him along the trails, and he had
run hard to stay ahead, breaking out of the woods just in front
of them. They'd caught up with him on the open sunlit field
and crossed the finish line first. Jamie's time for that race had
set a state record.

Since then, he'd heard them at most of his races, and if it
was rainy, he could sometimes smell their wet fur. But he'd
never seen them. And although he was unsure if they were
real or imagined (no one else seemed to notice them), he was
no longer afraid. Now he greeted them as friends. He relaxed
a bit. It would be a good race. He wasn't alone after all.

Jamie had told his mom about the wolves when she was
sick—not because they bothered him, but because he thought
she'd like the story. As she listened, her eyes held their old

fire. When she spoke, her voice, though sad, was strong. "Of course they run with you, Jamie—they are your family." She paused for a moment, and then spoke again with difficulty. "I should have known they would find you. Jamie, love, don't tell your dad about them just yet."

"My family? What do you mean?" He didn't know what he'd expected her to say, but it wasn't that.

She mumbled something about the flute music she was studying, then drifted off into the restless dreams that had occupied so much of her time in the days before she died.

Jamie was sure he felt a slight nip at his ankle as the starting gun went off.

Arriving home after the race, Jamie was surprised to see his father's car in the driveway. Too bad Dad didn't make the meet, he thought, but at least I won't have to search the bottom of my backpack for the key. The thrill of winning had warmed his spirits as he walked home, but the drizzle had turned to heavy rain, and he was glad to slip inside the unlocked back door.

As he kicked off his wet shoes, he was surprised again. The fragrances of ginger, garlic, and hot peppers filled the house, a pungent contrast to the damp, heavy air he'd left behind. His father stood at the stove, peering into a large, cast-iron wok.

"It smells like mandoo," said Jamie, hoping it was. He loved the spicy cabbage-and-meat dumplings.

"Come and catch the steam, it's the—"

"'The spirit of the food,' I remember," replied Jamie.

This was an old family joke, at least as far as he and his mother were concerned. Jamie always felt that his father actually believed it. Mealtimes were important to his dad. Even now, with just the two of them, he insisted they eat dinner together. (Although they seldom spoke anymore, and usually ate nothing more complicated than steamed rice and a bit of tofu—or pasta with a jar of tomato sauce if Jamie was cooking.) His dad must have spent all day on this meal.

It suddenly occurred to him that if his father had had time to cook, he could have come to the race. I bet he forgot all about it, thought Jamie. His sudden anger heated him at least as much as the steamy kitchen. His father, as though sensing the changed mood, looked up at him with a mix of hope and apprehension. A piece of scallion dangled from the left earpiece of his glasses, a large smudge of soy sauce darkened a cheek. Jamie sighed and walked toward the stove. He closed his eyes, bent his head to the pan, and took a long, deep breath. His father did the same.

Jamie headed upstairs, away from the sounds of rattling dishes and quiet whistling. Bits of melodies followed him, but Jamie didn't need to hear much to recognize what they were: fragments of the ancient song cycles that his mother had been reconstructing before she died. She had been working to establish a link between the music of the ancient Mongols and the indigenous tribes of the Pacific Northwest. She told Jamie that she was sure if she looked hard enough, she could find the trail back through time. His mom followed words and rhythms the way Hansel and Gretel followed bread crumbs.

She always had a song or a story to share, or even just a single word that seemed to hold infinite mysteries. For her, all language was full of links and patterns, which, if correctly interpreted, would provide her with a map to the world. But this last project was different. She was restrained, almost reluctant, about beginning the work. And then, once she began, she pursued it with an obsession that frightened Jamie.

He went into his room, shut the door, turned on the light, and quickly pulled down his sock—nothing there, it wasn't even red. Jamie sat down on his bed and looked around, absentmindedly rubbing his ankle. A series of shelves circled the room, one about knee level, a second hip high, and a third just below his shoulder. The top two shelves were covered with rocks, lined up like carts in a caravan, each carefully labeled. The bottom shelf was full of a jumbled mass of unsorted stones that glittered in the lamplight. There were rocks that could be arrowheads, could be fossils, could be crystals, could be meteors, could be geodes. Every rock could be magic as far as Jamie was concerned.

His mother had often gotten upset with him about the amount of clutter barely contained by his bedroom walls.

"This room will spawn life if you don't clean," she would say in a threatening tone. But even as a young child Jamie was secretly enchanted by the thought of a new life form rising up out of his rocks; life with two scholars could be a little dull, and he had never had a pet of any kind.

For as long as Jamie could remember, he had loved rocks. When he was little, he filled his pockets with them. His mom bought him books to study, and his dad brought the occasional geology professor home from the university to check out Jamie's collection.

Jamie reminded himself that his dad had been interested once. Maybe he hadn't told his father about the track meet. Or maybe his dad just hadn't realized how much Jamie would have liked him there. They really hadn't talked much lately. In fact, he didn't even know what project his father was working on now. Conference proceedings and research papers weren't the best bedtime stories, but at one time Jamie had been happy to fall asleep to the sound of his father's voice lovingly detailing a series of boring facts about the archaeological history of *Canis lupus*, the common wolf. Although, as far as his father was concerned, they were anything but common. Jamie thought about the nip to his ankle and had to agree.

"Don't tell your father about them just yet." Jamie recalled what his mother had said about the wolves. Now, as he walked downstairs, he wished he hadn't listened to her. He hoped it wasn't too late to get to know his father again.

Jamie slid into a chair. His father had put both forks and chopsticks on the table. Jamie picked up the chopsticks, fumbling slightly but determined to use them. He had his mother's long nose and golden eyes, although they were angled above high cheekbones like his father's. Not really one thing or the other, thought Jamie, not fork or chopsticks. "You have the face of a Mongol warrior," his father had insisted when Jamie was younger, prancing around with his young son on his shoulders. He'd told Jamie the stories about the Mongols' legendary ancestor, a fierce blue wolf that had roamed the steppes and mountain trails. The wolf's descendants still bore blue marks across their lower backs as a reminder of him. Jamie rubbed his spine—it was true, many Asians did have the spots. His own, though now faded, confirmed his heritage.

"Dad. *Ah-ba*." He added the Korean term his father preferred. Then he paused, trying to decide what to say about the mysterious letter.

"Ja-mie," replied his father, as usual splitting the syllables into distinct words. "Ja Mie Park." The way his father said it, it sounded as though it were a place somewhere in a strange city. Maybe the name does sound weird to him, thought Jamie. After all, he still calls himself Park Dai-Jeong, placing his family name first in the traditional Korean manner.

He looked into his father's eyes and saw his own loneliness and longing mirrored there. He saw something else as well: an envelope in his father's shirt pocket covered with the spidery script that was already very familiar.

"Jamie?" repeated his father.

Jamie grabbed a dumpling with his fingers and popped it into his mouth, chewing furiously in hopes of buying a little time. His father stared. Jamie waited for him to correct his manners, or to show him yet again the proper way to hold the chopsticks. But his father had a sweet half smile curving beneath his large glasses. "You eat like a wolf, Jamie." He tapped his shirt pocket in a contemplative manner and then pulled out the letter, placing it faceup on the table. "I have made my decision. You will do well there, I think. But I am told the choice is yours." His father looked at him expectantly.

Jamie choked on the dumpling. He had no idea what was going on. His father's smile widened. "But perhaps you would like me to help you decide?" He slid the letter across the table and looked at his son. Jamie nodded. Dai-Jeong went on, "A colleague of mine requires an assistant for the summer. Mostly daily chores. As I understand it, you would have free time to pursue your own interests as well."

"Do you mean rocks or running?" asked Jamie.

"Well," said his father, "Louise lives at the base of a mountain, and if you want to run to its rocky cliffs from her cabin each day, I think it would be okay."

"Louise?" Jamie was perplexed. "You called her a colleague—

but she signed her letter to me 'Aunt Louise.'"

"Your aunt—hmmm." His father looked briefly thoughtful, then smiled again. "Yes, yes, I hadn't thought of it before, but that's exactly what she is."

Jamie was trying to decide how to answer this confusing comment when a sudden wind rammed the rain against the glass.

"Ahh," said his father. "That will be her now. Will you go and get the door?"

Jamie walked to the front hall. He knew that he hadn't heard anybody knock. He opened the door anyway. "No one here, Dad," he called.

The wind slammed the door shut. A rich musical laugh mingled with his father's familiar chuckle. "It's all right, Jamie. Louise appears to have let herself in the back."

By the time he returned to the dining room, Louise had sat down. Using a single chopstick, she had speared a dumpling and was nibbling at the crisped edges. "Good," she said, in response to a raised eyebrow from Jamie's dad. "Really good. You were always a great cook, Dai-Jeong." Her voice was as vibrant as her laugh, with a rough quality that reminded Jamie of the smoky smell that lingered on her letter.

She finished the dumpling and turned to look at Jamie. He had been staring at her and, though flustered, did not look away. Her eyes, the same unusual shade of gold as his own, glittered behind a pair of large glasses. She was dressed simply in a bulky brown sweater and a long brown skirt. She had thrown some kind of shawl or muffler over her shoulders. It too was brown, as was the tangled mass of her rather wet hair. She appeared to be about his father's age, but there was a wildness about Louise.

After a moment or two, Louise looked away, gracefully maneuvering her chopstick toward another dumpling. "Did you get my letter, Jamie? Have you decided? Mmm, these are good," she said as she chewed. "I hope you'll come. Although I should tell you, I don't cook as well as your father."

Jamie glanced at his dad, who looked rather forlorn. Jamie wondered if it would be wrong to leave him alone for the summer. Louise quickly stabbed two more dumplings while his dad wasn't looking. She winked at Jamie, and he laughed in spite of himself.

"Dai-Jeong," she said, "what do you think?"

"I will miss him should he go. But you are right, it is time."

Louise shrugged. "What have you told him?"

Dai-Jeong cleared his throat; he seemed to be speaking with difficulty. "Only that he would be your assistant. That's what you said."

"Ahh, yes. That's right," replied Louise. Turning back to Jamie, she looked at him expectantly. "Well?"

Jamie looked at the two of them. Time? Time for what? "I have some questions," he stammered.

Louise waved her hand. "Yes, of course. You'll be paid."

"That's not what I meant," said Jamie, but as he spoke, he remembered what he had been doing to make money: baby-sitting for the mischievous four-year-old twin girls who lived next door. It *would* be nice to get away from them. He looked up to see both Louise and his father staring at him. "I might go."

"Excellent!" chortled Louise. "Go and pack. We'll leave when you're ready." The wind rattled the windows again. She grabbed the last dumpling.

Jamie looked at his father and felt his heart sink. "Now? What about school?"

"It's taken care of," said his father. "I spoke with the principal this afternoon. She will make arrangements with your teachers regarding your grades. And running is over for the season, is it not?"

Jamie stiffened. Dai-Jeong *had* known about the meet. He'd wanted to talk with his dad, but it seemed as though his father wanted to get rid of him. "Fine, I'll go," snapped Jamie as he shoved himself away from the table. His chair crashed to the floor. "You don't care anyway!" He ran up the stairs to his bedroom.

Jamie turned on the light and threw himself on the bed. He was angry and confused. His mother's death, his loneliness at school, his father's distance, the strange woman with whom he had agreed to spend the summer: He didn't know how to deal with any of these things. It was too much. He began to cry.

Some time later there was a soft knock at the door. Jamie ignored it, but his dad came in and stood by the bed. "Jamie, please. I can't think of how else to do this. I hope you will understand." He reached out and stroked his son's cheek. *"Sa rang hae yo,"* he murmured. "I love you." He rested his hand on Jamie's shoulder. Jamie pulled away. "Pack warm clothes. You'll need them," Dai-Jeong said as he left the room.

Jamie grabbed a duffel bag and quickly stuffed it with jeans, running clothes, some T-shirts, and socks. He dumped schoolbooks out of his backpack and onto the floor, then placed a cloth roll of chisels, a small folding shovel, and a magnifying glass in the empty bag. He fingered the rock-identification guides that had been gifts from his mother, finally choosing one thick volume and a small, battered paperback. He shoved his field journals, goggles, and a pair of work gloves in the pack's outer pockets, and strapped his sleeping bag to the bottom panel. Remembering his father's words, he reluctantly slipped on his down parka.

At the door he turned and looked around. His eyes again filled with tears. Going back into the room, he picked up his pile of schoolbooks, smoothing the crumpled pages. He stacked them neatly on the desk next to a small, framed photograph of himself taken when he was maybe two or three years old. It showed him holding a chunk of smoky quartz as big as his head, a beaming parent standing at each elbow. Finding that particular rock was one of his earliest memories.

He wrapped the photo in a pair of boxer shorts that had been draped over his desk chair and stuffed the bundle into the inner pocket of his jacket. You never know what you'll need, he thought as he grabbed his bags and walked downstairs.

Louise had thrown the shawl around her head and was standing near the door. Her glasses were a little crooked. "I'll go start the car. It may need a bit of convincing in this weather. I'm so glad you're coming with me, Jamie. I'm not used to driving in the city—I'll be happy for your eyes."

Jamie watched her step outside. He hoped she was joking about her driving. His chest felt tight, as though he had run a race. "Dad." Fear and worry made his voice quaver. "Dad?" He must be waiting by the car, thought Jamie as he followed Louise. An old brown Volvo was parked in front of the house. He didn't see his father.

"Ready for takeoff?" asked Louise. She laughed as she climbed into the car. "The back doors don't work; neither does the trunk. You'll need to throw your gear over the seat." She pushed open the passenger door, which squealed loudly.

"But my dad . . . "

"He told me to say good-bye for him." She paused before continuing in a quieter voice, "I think he left something on the seat for you."

Jamie tossed his pack and duffel bag back and climbed in, his legs brushing something warm. In the dim light he recognized one of the lacquered wooden boxes his father used for storing food. The spicy smell of mandoo filled the car. Jamie picked up the box. It was tied with a tasseled silk cord that held the lid in place, and slipped under the knot was a piece of folded paper. He fingered the string, then turned to shove the box onto the seat behind him.

"Ahh, no, Jamie. I don't think you want to put those dumplings back there."

The wind and rain were loud, but Jamie thought he heard the sound of panting nearby. The car started with a series of shudders followed by a sudden lurch forward. Dai-Jeong was standing in the open doorway, both hands outstretched. Jamie couldn't make out the expression on his face, but the light from the hallway outlined his dark form like a single tree on a moonlit hill.

Chamomile

CHAPTER 2

My Son,

Trust Louise. I wish we would have had
more time to talk, although I do not know
how I could have explained her to you. Once
you have figured things out, I think you will
understand. There was not enough time to
eat, either, so I have sent mandoo. If you
need me, call. I will hear you and come, no
matter where you are.

Jamie angled the sheet of paper so that it caught the green glow
of the fluorescent lights. He was struggling to make out the

meaning of the long series of geometric characters at the bottom of the note. Were they Korean? Not exactly—although maybe his dad had written them in a hurry. He'd try reading them again later, in the daylight.

He looked up as Louise came out of the gas station. She walked right in front of a large truck that was pulling up to the pump. The attendant hollered, the driver slammed on his brakes, Louise waved. Climbing into the Volvo, she tripped over the shawl. Her glasses fell off and caught on the steering wheel. She peered sternly into the backseat, then turned and smiled at Jamie. "Ready?"

Jamie looked behind him. The seat was empty except for his stuff. He slouched against the door and moaned. Trust Louise—no way! Why had his father wanted him to go with her? He folded the note and slipped it back under the silken cord. His stomach growled, but he knew that if he opened the box, it would be Louise who ate the dumplings. As though reading his thoughts, she glanced at the box and sniffed.

Jamie stared out the window and tried to ignore her. The rain had stopped. In the moonlight he could see that there were more trees and fewer houses. He tried to figure out which direction they were headed. North, he decided, and maybe inland a bit, although he wasn't sure. What was it his father had written in the note? " . . . no matter where you are." Even allowing for Dai-Jeong's formal and sometimes incorrect English, the wording was very strange.

Jamie fiddled with the knotted ends of the silk string. It had always been hard for him to talk with his father. The work Dai-Jeong did in the lab was more real to him than what went on around Seattle. When Jamie had been younger, he had feared that his dad, always lost in his own thoughts, would get hit by a car. He's like Louise, Jamie thought, glancing in her direction. They're both in another world.

Again he wondered what the connection was between the two of them. Aunt? Jamie shook his head. She certainly wasn't his father's sister. Maybe his mother's—they had the same color eyes. He remembered how his mother had referred to the wolves as "family." He remembered too the argument his parents had had the evening after he'd told her about them. His mother's voice was weak, but her final words were unmistakable: "I don't want him to go." Jamie tightened his grip on the enameled box.

"Jamie, open it," Louise murmured gently. "The dumplings won't keep, and we have a long way to go." He undid the cord and slipped it and the note into his coat pocket. He opened the box and wedged it behind the stick shift. "You better go first Jamie—I'm partial to your dad's cooking." They ate in silence. Jamie felt better with something in his stomach. They reached for the last dumpling at the same time. Louise laughed, and Jamie smiled at her shyly. "No, you take it," she said reluctantly, and then added, "You know, there is more than one way for a parent to say I love you."

Jamie fell asleep sometime near dawn. He woke when the car hit a deep gully on the side of the road, bounced down the face of a shallow ravine, and ground to a stop. The sun was already low in the sky. He must have slept for hours.

Louise was beaming. "Well, here we are, Jamie-boy. Home. I'll back the car out later. Grab your stuff and come with me." She jumped out and tried pushing the door shut. When it wouldn't close, she left it open, walking briskly down a narrow path that disappeared in a small grove of black pines. Her shawl had caught on the lower branches of one of the trees and slipped from her shoulders. She continued on without it. She was singing. In spite of his reservations about her sanity, the joy in her voice made Jamie smile.

He took a deep breath. The air was cool and smelled like pine. Good for running, he thought, zipping his jacket. A low mountain rose just beyond the trees, its surface a rumpled brown that glistened with flecks of pink and gray and khaki— a summer's worth of rocks. Here and there he saw clusters of the large wood-ear mushrooms Dai-Jeong bought at the Korean groceries in Seattle.

The thought of his father made him suddenly lonely. He grabbed his bags and hurried after Louise. He stopped to pick up her shawl, heard panting nearby, and decided to leave it where it was. I'm as crazy as she is, he thought, quickening his pace to a trot.

The path was well traveled. It curved through the pines

before opening out at the edge of a broad clearing surrounded
by trees. A few small wooden sheds of assorted sizes were scattered across the open space; a large fenced vegetable garden
flanked one side, an orchard another. Here and there, flowers
bloomed in unplanned clusters, and birds swooped from the
trees to the ground and back again. Louise was already seated
on the doorstep of one of the buildings. Jamie guessed that
this was her house despite the small size: It had windows and
a chimney.

"Well, what do you think?" she asked, waving her hand
around.

"Uh, great."

It was obvious that whatever he thought, Louise believed
this was paradise. She stretched her legs and sighed with
pleasure before standing. "I don't know about you, but I'm
starving. Let's get something to eat." Instead of going inside,
she picked up a couple of baskets stacked near the steps and
handed one to Jamie. "Animal, vegetable, or mineral?"

Jamie looked at her in confusion. "What?"

"I'm sorry," she replied, laughing. "Do you want to gather
eggs or vegetables? Or rocks? I hear you like them—we could
have stone soup."

Jamie eyed her with misgiving. She looked as though she
meant it.

"Come on," she called as she started walking. "Today we'll
do it together."

One of the sheds had an attached pen that contained a number of chickens. They started cackling as Louise unhooked the gate. "I need to keep them in when I'm not around; there are wolves here."

Jamie shuddered at the mention of wolves. Imagining them in Seattle was one thing, but something about picturing them in this place, surrounded by wilderness, made him a little nervous.

"There are wolves, but they won't hurt you."

He followed her into the pen without comment. She slipped her hand here and there, pulling eggs from the mounds of straw. She reminded Jamie of a magician pulling rabbits from a hat. While she worked, she commended the chickens for their efforts. The hens, puffed up and squawking, followed her out into the yard and across the clearing to the garden. Louise pushed through the gate, keeping up her compliments, now directed at the early lettuces, peas, chives, and sorrel.

Jamie, left holding the basket of eggs, was impressed in spite of himself. The garden was as disorganized and unruly as Louise, but it also had something of her offbeat charm. Again she did the magician bit, poking her hand around in first one clump of sprouts and then another, swift and sure amid the chaos. After a few minutes she straightened up and took a deep breath. Turning to the mountain, she bowed her head, but not so low as to keep Jamie from noting her smile of contentment.

He looked down at his basket so that she wouldn't see him staring. Here in the sunlight he noticed what the shadows of the chicken coop had hidden. The eggs were beautiful: pale blue, smoke gray, turquoise, mossy green. Jamie, used to the white, perfectly matched ovals from the food store, caught his breath with a whistle.

Louise looked up at him, the smile lingering on her face. "Wait till you taste them. Here, look at these." She held out her basket.

Jamie recognized rhubarb, asparagus, spinach, and— "Flowers?" he squeaked. "We're not going to eat flowers?" He clutched his stomach.

Louise laughed. "Soon we'll have strawberries, but this will do for now." She headed for the cabin, but instead of going inside, she placed the basket of vegetables on the step and picked up a couple of large buckets. With one looped over each arm, she walked to a pump a couple of yards away and, settling them on the ground, she began pumping. Jamie was surprised at how strong she was, and competent, given her seemingly haphazard approach to everything. She filled the second bucket. He suddenly realized that she must be doing this because the cabin lacked running water. And if it lacked running water . . .

"That's right," she said. "Right over there." She waved her hand toward the smallest and most distant shed. Louise started humming again as she carried the buckets inside. He went to explore the privy.

When Jamie rejoined Louise, she was starting a fire in a woodstove that stood against the back wall. Jamie looked around the one-room cabin. There was a large window in each of the side walls, and two smaller windows flanked the doorway. A ladder, propped near the woodstove, led to what appeared to be to a small loft of some kind. The walls were plaster, tinted a rich ocher like butterscotch candy, or like the color of Louise's eyes, he thought.

A strange wall color. But he had to admit, it looked good as a backdrop to Louise's eclectic possessions. Around the room, shelves held a variety of colorful pitchers and bowls. He noticed an unfamiliar pungent smell that he decided came from the bundles of herbs and dried flowers that hung from the ceiling. Other hooks held bits of ribbons and feathers. The low bed in one corner was piled with pillows and blankets. A patterned rug covered most of the floor, and stacks of books covered most of the rug.

"It looks as though you like to read." He bent down and picked up a familiar-looking volume. "My dad has this one."

Louise nodded and pushed another log into the fire. "I grew up here, but I studied in Seattle for a while. The books remind me of those days. I miss it sometimes." She pointed toward a basin set on the large table. "You can wash up a bit and then give me a hand cooking."

The water he splashed on his face was cold. He stood briefly by the woodstove and watched the flames through the small glass set into its door. Louise had placed vegetables on the table and was cracking eggs into a large cast-iron skillet. "Eggs and a salad tonight? I'm not the cook your father is, but you won't go hungry while you're here."

"I am hungry," said Jamie. "I can't believe I slept so long in the car. How far did we drive? Where are we, anyway?"

"You slept for quite a while." There was something guarded in her voice. She was quiet for a moment as she shook the pan back and forth on the top of the woodstove. "Jamie, you'll have questions, I think."

He snorted. That was an understatement.

She smiled at the expression on his face but replied seriously. "There will be things I cannot tell you, Jamie. But I will never lie. Trust me. Although at times this place—and what happens here—may seem strange to you, I hope you will become comfortable." She set the pan on the table. "It's ready—come and sit down. Then we'll talk."

Jamie slid into a wobbly chair. He sniffed, then took a tentative bite of the flower-strewn eggs Louise had served him. "Not bad," he admitted. "So, where are we?" he asked after a few more mouthfuls.

"North," replied Louise.

"Canada?" He took another bite.

"Nooo." Her voice was hesitant. "Do you think you would have slept through customs?" she added more confidently.

"Where then?"

"Near the border." She looked down at her plate.

"Are we still in Washington?"

"Near that border too." She grabbed their plates so quickly that Jamie, about to take another bite, stabbed the table with his fork. "I'll do clean-up tonight. Why don't you get ready for bed?"

"But Louise . . . "

"That's enough for tonight. You're up in the loft. I think you'll find everything you need." She whistled as she scraped the plates. She was clearly done with conversation.

Jamie grabbed his belongings and started up the ladder, trying to balance his bags in one hand and hang on with the other. After climbing a couple of rungs, he was able to peer into the small space. A futon tucked under the slope of the roof took up most of the floor. It was piled with nearly as many quilts and pillows as Louise's bed. He climbed onto the landing, stood up, and cracked his head on the low ceiling. Louise, hearing the thump, chuckled downstairs. "Not funny," he muttered.

A wardrobe with paneled doors was built into one end of the loft, a small window just fit into the other. Jamie placed his books on the floor near the futon, then propped the photograph of his parents against them. Changing his mind, he removed the photo from its frame and slipped the picture into his journal. I want it, he thought, I just don't want to look at it. He put the notes from Louise and his father in the notebook as well. Finally, he wiped the mandoo box clean with a T-shirt and put it next to the books. Too tired to unpack further, he crawled into bed and slept.

The next morning, as he looked down from his loft, he saw Louise at the table. Her hair was full of bits of bark and bracken. She looked up, not quite focusing on him at first, but then her eyes began to glisten behind the oversize glasses. "Delighted!" she trilled. "Jamie, I'm absolutely delighted that you're here. You look a little ragged—did you sleep in those clothes?" She looked at him questioningly. After a moment she shrugged. "Never mind. What does it matter now? I've got some pajamas you can wear tonight. In the meantime, you know where things are. When you come back, we'll talk some more."

I'm ragged, he thought. She's the one with all the stuff in her hair. He thought of asking her where she'd been. But he stepped out into the clearing, his questions less compelling than his desire to find the outhouse. When he reached the door, he hopped up and down on his bare feet, trying to convince himself to go inside. "I should have worn shoes," he grumbled as he left the shadowy interior of the privy a few minutes later. After washing his hands and face (and rinsing his feet) in the icy water from the pump, he went into the cabin and joined Louise at the table.

He watched her drink coffee, eyes closed, leaning back in her chair. "Aunt Louise . . . " he hesitated.

"Puhleez, just Louise." She started to chuckle.

"Why is everything always so funny?"

"You know—*Please, Louise*—it rhymes."

"Okay. Louise. Are you really my aunt?"

"I am indeed," she said without any explanation. "Would you like a cup of coffee?" Not waiting for an answer, she poured a mug of thick, oily coffee. "Do you take milk?"

"Maybe just milk."

"No sugar?"

"No." He wrinkled his nose. "No coffee."

She looked briefly startled, then smiled. "That's funny. But I'm not going to laugh." She emptied his mug into her own. "I think I have some powdered milk I can make for you to have with your breakfast."

Jamie noticed some crumbs and a jam-covered knife on the table, but he saw no other food.

"Oh." She seemed flustered. "Did I eat it all? I'm not used to company yet. How about an egg?"

While she was cooking him an omelette, Jamie took out his field notebook and quickly wrote:

> *Eat whenever there is food.*
> *Sleep in socks.*
> *Don't drink water before going to bed.*

*Don't drink the coffee—ever—it looks like
mud and smells like tar.*

Louise set down his plate. "Keeping a journal? That's nice. They are very useful things."

Jamie covered the page with his arm. He didn't want to hurt her feelings.

"Eat up. Then we'll go find something exciting to write about."

He wasn't sure what she meant, but by the end of the morning Jamie was too tired to care. Under Louise's supervision he had gathered eggs, cleaned out the chicken coop, turned the compost piles, fixed the latch on the garden gate, and cut some wood. He also tried to weed the garden. "Not those," she said as he started to pull out the dandelions. "Not those either, that's sheep sorrel—good for the bones."

He glanced at her, his fingers above a prickly plant his neighbor had routinely excavated from her roses.

"Ahh, that's nettle. Leave it right where it is."

Jamie sat back on his heels.

"Hmph." Louise narrowed her eyes. "Maybe enough work for one day. Why don't you go and explore the mountain?"

"Alone?" Jamie was apprehensive.

"Well." She waved her hand toward the path. "You can't miss it. And as for the way back, I'm sure you'll find your way. Have fun." She walked behind the cabin.

Her comments didn't make Jamie any less nervous, but the prospect of checking out the mountain for rocks overcame his reservations. He went to the loft and organized tools and notebooks in his pack. There was no sign of Louise when he came outside, so he shouted a good-bye and started off. He had run about halfway to the mountain when he realized two things: He hadn't had any lunch, and she hadn't answered any questions.

Jamie was enjoying himself too much to care. He followed a well-worn trail through the woods, keeping the mountain more or less in front of him. Louise was right—this part was easy. A thick layer of pine needles cushioned his steps and muffled the sound of his feet. He quickly lost himself to the rhythm of the run, not really paying attention to where he was. He didn't notice the gradual change in the terrain, and was startled to suddenly see a rocky cliff rise up in front of him. "Oh wow." The earth shimmered. "It might not be such a bad summer."

He scrambled partway up the sloped talus. Good, not too steep to climb. He scuffed the surface with his toe, loosening a number of small rocks that skittered downhill. He knelt, brushed some sand aside, and studied the surface. He took out his field book and jotted a few descriptive details. He scraped at the ground. Rubbed some dirt between his fingers. Made a few more notes. He was very methodical. With two months ahead of him, he could afford to take his time.

Jamie moved back and forth across the cliff, stopping now and then to smear a soil sample on the page or sketch an interesting rock formation. He lost himself in his work the same way he lost himself in his running, sadness and confusion temporarily at bay. At one point, he stood and stretched. His stomach rumbled. Jamie looked up and was surprised to see the sun had dropped quite low. I should head back, he thought. If I'm not there in time, she'll probably eat my dinner. He packed his tools, scrambled back down the talus to the tree line, and realized he couldn't see the trail.

At first he jogged along the edge of the woods, thinking he had just missed the entrance somehow. When that failed, he climbed back up the cliff and tried retracing his footsteps. But he had crisscrossed his own path numerous times, and the wind, which now whipped sand into his face, had erased most of his tracks. He fought to stay calm.

Scanning the sky, he tried to remember where the sun had been when he'd arrived. He couldn't. "Not that that would do me any good," he muttered. Maybe Louise would teach him how to read the sky; she would know. Louise! Jamie shook his head. He couldn't count on her. She might not even notice that he was gone. This thought totally unnerved him. "Louise!" he shouted. "Louise! Louise!" His voice echoed.

It began to grow dark. Jamie again ran back and forth along the tree line, fear as much as exertion making his breathing quick and raspy. His hands and face were damp with sweat despite the cool evening air. He ran faster, gasping now, long, ragged breaths. At first he nearly missed the other noise. He stopped and listened: a slight snorting, a few distant yelps. The sounds drew closer. One wolf, maybe two.

They were at his heels. He couldn't see them. They rushed past. It didn't make sense, but he knew enough to follow. He scrambled across the rocks, nearly falling as the muffled barks drew away from him again. Jamie ran in pursuit, arriving at the entrance to the trail as the yelps faded into the deeper darkness of the woods. He picked up his pace and quickly found his way back to the clearing.

Before he could even catch his breath, Louise emerged from the trees behind him. Why hadn't he seen her? Her hair was tousled, her shirt scattered with leaves. She held two large trout in her arms, although she carried no fishing rod.

"You're late."

"I got lost." He thought he heard something in the bushes.

"Ready for dinner?" Louise asked. "Or maybe a shower?" she added, wrinkling her nose.

He opened his mouth to speak, but Louise was already walking away.

"Over by the garden," she called. "I think you'll like it."

He looked in the direction she pointed and saw something hanging from the limb of an apple tree, horizontal rays of the evening sun glinting off its surface. As he walked closer, he could see a large plastic bag, filled with water, hooked to the tree. A nozzled tube dangled from one corner. He reached up, his hand brushing the bag. "Hot!" he said in surprise. Folded over another limb were a towel and the promised pajamas. How had she managed this? he wondered. He stripped to his boxers, hesitated briefly, and with a furtive look toward the cabin, removed them as well.

He grabbed the hose and turned a small valve, directing the sudden flow of warm water toward his face. Working quickly, he rinsed off and wrapped the towel around his waist. He eyed the pajamas suspiciously. Printed with neon astronauts, they appeared to be the right size for a space capsule. But it was cold, and he'd worn the same clothes for forty-eight hours. He pulled on the bottoms and tripped, catching his foot in the extra length. I'm as clumsy as Louise, he thought, and looked up to see her in the doorway of the cabin.

She shrugged. "Well, I couldn't be sure of the size. Better too big than too small, though. And I thought the pattern was appropriate."

"Astronauts?"

"That's right." She nodded. "This must seem like another planet. Right?"

Jamie gasped. That was exactly what he thought of this place. How did she know?

"I found them in Seattle, when I was waiting to pick you up. The shower bag too. The water is solar heated. I usually bathe in the river, but you're a city kid and . . ."

Jamie didn't know if he should glare at her or thank her.

"Lacks a bit in the way of privacy, though," she continued without waiting for him to answer. "Maybe you can build some kind of enclosure tomorrow. Now it's time to eat." She turned and went back into the cabin. He quickly pulled on the pajama tops, picked up his clothes, and hurried after her. He wanted to ask a few more questions, and the trout smelled wonderful.

Comfrey &
Crow Garlic

CHAPTER 3

Eat whenever there is food.
Sleep in socks.
Don't drink water before going to bed.
Don't drink the coffee—ever.

To the list he'd started yesterday Jamie added: "Mark the trail." Then he turned the page and started sketching out plans for the shower enclosure. Occasionally he glanced out the loft's small window at the mountain. A faint morning haze lingered around its summit, but here and there he could glimpse patches of sky that were a brilliant blue.

"No," Louise had answered yesterday when he had asked if

it rained as much as it did in Seattle. "No, not by half." It was one of the only direct answers she had given him since he'd arrived, despite his numerous questions. Still, the prospect of nice weather did make him feel better about spending the summer away from home. And strange as it was here, he couldn't help but feel excited about digging rocks.

With that thought in mind, he swung his legs over the edge of the futon, stepped on the extra fabric of the pajamas, and fell, cracking his knee on the floor. Jumping up, he smacked his head on the low ceiling, groaned, and fell back to the futon.

"Jamie? You okay? Breakfast is ready."

"I'll be right there." He rubbed his head. Careful to stay low, he changed into jeans and a T-shirt and began to crawl toward the edge of the loft. But a sudden thought made him turn around and open his notebook again. Grabbing his pen, he wrote:

Do not wear pajamas.

And then, very carefully, he climbed down the ladder.

"I left your pancakes over on the stove. Didn't trust myself. Coffee?"

He shook his head.

"Oh, that's right, just milk." She filled a mug from the pitcher on the table.

He took a large gulp and looked up in surprise. It was

delicious, so fresh it tasted almost wild. "This is good."

"So is my coffee," she replied, pretending to be affronted. "It's goat's milk."

Jamie looked at her quizzically. He knew it hadn't been there yesterday. "Where did it come from?" He took a bite of pancake.

She waved her hand toward the door. "A neighbor." She quickly stood and began to clear the dishes.

He continued to chew. He hadn't seen any goats, and he hadn't seen any neighbors. He swallowed. "Which direction?"

"I'm sure you'll meet them. Some other time." Louise sat back down with another cup of coffee. "Today I thought I might ask you to take over the feeding and care of the chickens, and chopping wood. I think I'll do the weeding." She winked at him. "About the shower, what did you come up with?" She glanced at his notebook.

He opened to his sketches, eager to show her the designs. Then he realized that he hadn't told her he'd been working on ideas for the enclosure. Looking up, he caught her eye, then raised his own brows in an unspoken question.

"Well." She shrugged. "I heard your pencil. And it sounded too scratchy to be writing. Jamie—I'm used to living alone. Or at least, used to living without other people." She cleared her throat. "I have to pay attention to what goes on around me, eh? And to know what the plants and animals are telling me, even though they might not speak."

Jamie thought about the panting wolves and stiffened slightly. Louise seemed not to notice. She took one of his pancakes, nibbled at it a bit, and kept talking. "I expect it's hard to understand, but think about your rocks. I'm sure you know what lies beneath the surface even before you've started digging. You look at the soil, the terrain, the lay of the land. Other things too, I bet. Things that you've learned through practice and experience that would be hard to explain. Right?"

Jamie nodded. He knew exactly what she meant. He had tried to tell other kids about talking to the rocks. But after one or two strange glances from them, he'd always given up. Now Louise had explained it perfectly.

"Sure, there are surprises," she went on. "But what would life be like without a little mystery? Let's see the sketches." She stood up to move her chair closer to his, bumped her coffee cup, tried to grab it before it spilled, and in the process knocked her chair to the floor. Jamie's left hand shot out to snatch his notebook from the widening puddle of coffee. His right hand reached for Louise's arm, steadying her until she regained her balance.

"Good reflexes." She wasn't at all distressed by the incident. "We'll get along well together."

Jamie looked up and studied his aunt. Louise's hair was standing on end, her glasses were crooked, and coffee stains spattered the front of her shirt. Somewhat to his surprise he realized he agreed with her. "You know," he admitted, "I think you're right."

While they cleaned up, Jamie described his plans for the shower. He'd seen a small stand of willow near the garden. It reminded him of a trip he had taken with his parents years ago—in fact, the trip when he'd been photographed with the large piece of smoky quartz. They had stopped near a stream to picnic, and Jamie had wanted to dig for rocks in the shallow water. Dai-Jeong had cut willow switches from trees growing near the bank and quickly woven the flexible branches into a small flat basket for his son to use as a sieve. Jamie explained this to Louise now. "Anyway," he added, "I thought I could make some kind of lean-to out of your willows to enclose the shower."

She looked at him for a moment before speaking. "I taught your father to weave those baskets. We were very young."

Jamie was startled. "How long have you known my dad?" He had assumed that if Louise really was his aunt, the connection must be through his mother's family. And Dai-Jeong hadn't even come from Korea until . . . when was it? Jamie tried to remember.

Louise continued without answering him, "Yes, it's a good plan. Can you weave it in place, though? Without cutting them? They're very flexible. I use the willow bark for tea sometimes. Did you know it's full of salicylic acid? The same stuff that makes aspirin work so well."

Jamie, distracted by her comments, nodded. "My dad told me that too, I planned to do it that way." He opened his notebook. "Besides, the leaves will help screen the, umm, the view." He blushed a bit. "And I thought I could dig a trench so the runoff flowed into the garden."

"Very clever!" Louise studied his drawings. "Go ahead and start on it. But first feed the chickens."

They worked outdoors for the rest of the morning. Jamie patiently wove the supple young willow shoots into a three-sided, chest-high screen. Louise offered an occasional suggestion but mostly seemed content to work in the garden, leaving him to make his own decisions. Getting the drainage to flow in the direction he wanted was more difficult; it took a seemingly endless number of water buckets carried from the pump and a lot of rerouting of the drainage ditch. When he finally got it right, he stretched, hands on his back. He was muddy, a little sore, and very pleased with the work he had done. The sun was overhead. He scanned the sky briefly, looking for something, although he wasn't sure what.

"Rocks calling?" Louise asked. "Go ahead. There are some biscuits on the table if you're hungry."

Jamie nodded. Suddenly he *was* hungry, and he did want to go to the mountain—although he was a little nervous about getting back afterward. Going into the cabin, he got his things from the loft, and the biscuits from the table. Louise had wrapped them in a long strip of red cloth. I wonder why she used this, he thought, fingering the silky fabric. A gust of wind blew through the open door and the cloth fluttered. "It's just the thing to mark the trail, though," he said to himself, his shoulders relaxing slightly. He hadn't wanted to admit, even to himself, how apprehensive he was about finding his way home from the mountain.

And then he shook his head. Louise must have left the fabric there on purpose. He frowned, still a bit disconcerted by her ability to anticipate his thoughts. Any lingering resentment was forgotten, however, when after a long and enjoyable afternoon on the mountain, he brushed the crumbs of the last chive-and-goat-cheese biscuit from his hands, packed up his tools, and trotted toward the red cloth tied to a tree branch near the entrance to the trail.

After the first few weeks at Louise's house, Jamie learned to keep his head low as he rolled out of bed, to keep his shoes near the edge of the futon, and to assume that Louise would answer, at best, one question out of ten. She made vague references to her "work," and occasionally she would sit at the table surrounded by journals and books. Among them, to Jamie's surprise, were a number of the books on wolves that his father owned. "Did you get all these books when you studied in Seattle?" he asked one evening.

She looked up from her papers. "Most of them." She started to write again.

"Do you miss it? The city, I mean."

"My work is here now. But yes, sometimes I miss the freedom to do as I please."

"Really? What could be more free than this?" He waited, but she said nothing more. Nor would she answer any more of his questions.

Jamie helped Louise with chores every morning. He and the old rooster, a rather battered specimen named Gus, would walk around the coop each morning. Jamie changed the straw and gathered eggs, while Gus squawked and nipped his hands. Then Gus would follow him to the compost heap and wood-pile. Every couple of days he and the rooster would walk to a nearby stream and wash clothes, carrying them back to Louise's cabin, where a line was strung between two trees. Gus crowed loudly throughout the entire process.

"I've had Gus for years, and he's never made this much noise," Louise complained one day.

Jamie defended his friend. "He's just supervising."

Louise sniffed and mumbled, "That's my job." But she seemed amused nonetheless.

Each night after dinner, Jamie did dishes by the pump. When he was done, he carefully poured the bucket of used water on the raspberry canes. Then he climbed up to the loft and wrote in his journal or read his field books. As the light of the long evenings of the northern summer finally faded to gray, he would crawl under the many blankets and fall asleep in his clothes. "After all, I'm clean enough," he said out loud the first time he did it, as though in response to some grown-up's raised eyebrow. And besides, he thought, with Louise in charge anything could happen; it was good to be prepared, even in the middle of the night. As for the astronaut pajamas, he folded them neatly and put them in the wardrobe, where they gradually became hidden by the rocks he brought home from the mountain.

It didn't matter. Louise never noticed what he slept in. Each morning, enjoying the illusion of flight, he jumped from the ladder when he was about halfway down—landing with a soft plop if it was a good jump, a thud if not. Louise smiled at the noise, but Jamie felt as though she were really somewhere else. She was distracted, quiet, fiddling with her coffee cup or picking leaves from her hair and clothes.

He learned to leave her alone in the mornings, to go about his chores quietly except for the occasional necessary question. Around midday Jamie looked for her, saying good-bye if he found her, penning up the chickens if she was gone. Then, after filling a water bottle from the pump, he ran down the trail. He was soon sure of the way home, but had left the red cloth tied to the tree. As for the wolves, he'd not heard them again. He decided he had imagined them, and was content to leave it at that for now.

When he returned to the cabin in the evenings, Louise

was more talkative. She was usually in the garden, and as he ran into the clearing, the tools in his pack jangling, she would look up and wave. They would sit on the cabin step then, and Louise would study his finds before they made dinner.

She had been right. She wasn't the cook his father was. She sang exuberantly off-key while she worked, banging a large cleaver against the cutting board in time to the music. Meals burned, pans boiled over, something always spilled. Still, the food here seemed more alive. There was often fish, always a salad. Sometimes a stew made from wild mushrooms, new potatoes the size of his thumb, and rabbit or grouse simmered on the stove. He wondered where she got the game. He saw no evidence of a gun and thought it unlikely that she would use one in any case. No, a longbow was more her style. But he hadn't seen one of those around either.

He'd asked her a couple of times where the food came from and she'd shrugged or said something vague about "the neighbors." Once, when he'd pestered her on the subject, she'd given him a withering look followed by a brief but convincing lecture on the idea that "the ancient and elegant relationship between hunter and prey was the basis for all contemporary dance." She poked her fork in the air as she spoke and then fixed Jamie with an expectant stare.

He nodded vigorously. "Yes, Aunt Louise." He didn't have a clue as to what she meant, but she looked as though she might bite him. He thought it best not to ask her about hunting again.

This wasn't unusual. Although she seldom answered his questions directly, their dinner-table discussions were frequently animated. Louise seemed to have passionate opinions about almost everything. And yet she also seemed more open to new ideas than many of the adults he knew. She had the same nonjudgmental curiosity that his father did, but Dai-Jeong had channeled it into his research, while Louise seemed more engaged by what happened around her.

One night, watching him chew some rhubarb stewed with honey, Louise laughed. "You always look so surprised when you bite into something. Is my cooking that shocking?"

"No." Jamie was embarrassed. "Well, maybe . . . yes. I'm surprised at how good it tastes."

Louise smiled, waved her hand toward the window, and tipped over her glass. "It's because it's real," she said, unfazed by the water dripping onto the floor. As Jamie scrambled to mop the spill with his napkin, she cocked her head as though waiting for a response.

She's nuts, thought Jamie, but I know what she means. After that, she let him help prepare dinner. Each night he did more, and did it more confidently. At last, to his great relief, Louise let him take over all the cutting and chopping. She had dropped the large cleaver close to his feet more than once.

"I never knew that rocks could be so beautiful," she commented one evening as they sat on the step. She was holding a piece of mica close to her large glasses. "There are rainbows gathered in its fissures. It seems almost alive." She sighed, handing the rock back to Jamie. She studied him for a moment with a serious look. "Jamie . . . " She paused. "Never mind," she continued in a lighter tone. "Go take your shower. Will you bring me some chives on the way in? And the radishes are ready if you want to pull a few. Oh," she added with a glint in her eye, "I may have left a raspberry or two."

"They're finally ripe?" Jamie jumped up, ran inside to get his clean clothes, and danced all the way to the shower. He had been waiting a long time to taste those raspberries, and he'd planted the radish seeds himself a few days after he'd arrived, amazed at how quickly the thin shoots had spiraled from the ground to the sky.

After washing, he stepped through the gate into the garden. He had gradually learned the names of most of the plants, especially the ones Louise grew for eating. And although she still wouldn't let him weed for fear that he would pull up one of the wild plants she used for healing, she trusted him enough to gather foods for dinner. He reached his hand into the damp soil and eased a large scarlet radish into the sunlight. It occurred to him that his enthusiasm for gardening would be considered "uncool" at home. He wondered, grinning to himself as he headed toward the house, what the kids would say if they knew how much he liked to cook.

"Just like your dad." Louise was watching Jamie slice the radishes. He winced at the comparison. Although he was enjoying the time at Louise's, he was still bothered by Dai-Jeong's abrupt good-bye—and his apparent lack of interest in Jamie's welfare. He didn't want to talk about his dad.

But Louise went on, "Why don't you write to him, Jamie? I can mail the letter next time I go for supplies. He'd love to hear from you. Describe this place through your eyes—tell him about where you run, and the rocks. He's been here often, you know."

Jamie rocked the knife up and down, the blade hitting the cutting board with a loud thwack, the nearly transparent slices of radish skittering onto the counter. He did not look at Louise. "You never talk about my mother, but my dad seems to come up in every conversation. When was he here? No one told me." He took a deep breath. "Aunt Louise," he said, his voice tight, "my father can write to me if he wants to know how I'm doing." He picked up another radish.

Louise reached out and took it from him, popping it into her mouth. "Jamie," she said as she chewed, apparently un-ruffled by his comments, "are you ever lonely? Have you seen anyone on the mountain?"

Jamie shrugged. He'd been tempted more than once to tell her about hearing the wolves the day he got lost. But now he was too upset.

Louise continued. "The rocks are lovely. As I said, they are almost alive—but not quite. Don't cut yourself off from other people." Her voice was serious, as it had been earlier.

Jamie, startled by the uncharacteristic note of sadness in her voice, began to reassure her that he was, in fact, not bothered by his solitary state. But before he could speak, she went on, "It isn't always easy to live alone. You should write to Dai-Jeong. It wasn't easy for him to let you come here. But Jamie, he felt it was time you got to know your family." She stared at him through her glasses.

Jamie turned away. He was angered by her insistence, and a little frightened by the way her golden eyes focused on him. He finished cooking in silence, then went to bed without eating anything, not even the raspberries. Later that night, when hunger woke him, he thought he heard her speaking with someone. He fell back asleep before he was sure.

Hawthorn

CHAPTER 4

Dear Dad,

Louise told me I had to write to you. So I am. Although I don't know why I'm listening to her. She is nuts, and never answers questions. But I guess I like her well enough.

What did the marks at the bottom of your note mean? I thought at first they were Korean, but they're not and I can't read them.

Jamie ripped the page from his notebook, crumpled it into a ball, and with a quick turn of his wrist, sent it flying. It landed on the ground near four other unfinished letters to his father that had received the same treatment. He scowled, then shouted at the sky, "Forget it, Louise! I don't care what you think." Gus, pecking near Jamie's feet, looked up and cocked his head. A chickadee flew from a branch of the nearest pine. Louise said nothing, because Louise wasn't there.

In fact, he had not seen her since his abrupt departure from the dinner table the evening before. She had not been there when he woke. And when he'd checked, the brown Volvo was gone from its spot out on the dirt road. Although he had stalled at the cottage until long after noon, she still had not returned. After finishing every chore he could think of, Jamie had started to write to his father. Maybe if he did what Louise wanted, she would come back. And he wanted her to come back. But everything he wrote looked wrong to him.

Jamie stood and stretched. He looked toward the mountain. Louise had left before, but never without telling him. Now he was reluctant to go without seeing her. Partly because he was worried and, he admitted to himself, partly because he was very hungry. He hadn't eaten anything since lunchtime yesterday. Finally he decided that he might as well run to the mountain. If the rocks failed to keep him from thinking of his hunger and her absence, he could at least pretend that she had returned while he was gone.

He went inside, grabbed his tools and field book, and stuffed a pen into his pocket. Then he started opening the cupboards in search of food. Jamie looked around in surprise at the sound of a faint bark near his heel. He hadn't heard the wolves for weeks, not since that first day on the mountain. He reached for a biscuit left over from last night's dinner and quickly dropped it. "Yeow!" he yelped, rubbing his ankle. There was no sign of a cut, but it sure felt as though he'd been bitten. He reached tentatively toward the biscuit and heard a warning growl. Quickly shoving his hands in his pockets, he stepped away from the platter. "Why can't I have one? I'm really hungry, and anyway, they're mine since I didn't eat them last night." The growl became a bit louder.

"Okay, okay," Jamie said. He hoisted his pack to his shoulder and stepped outside. As he pulled the door shut behind him, it resisted, as though a large object were in the way. Something seemed to brush past his leg; then the door slid easily into place. Jamie sighed, "Okay, so you're coming." Then he added in a resigned tone, "Still, if I'm the one making this up, I don't see why I can't eat."

He headed across the clearing, the thud of tools against his back not quite masking the heavy breathing of something he couldn't see. Louise's chickens had scattered around the clearing. Jamie glanced at them but decided that gathering them back into the coop would take too much time. And anyway, what harm could it do to leave them loose just this once? His escort grabbed his leg and flipped him to the ground. Suddenly he was lying in the dirt, eye to eye with Gus. "All right, all right," he called into the air. "I'll put the chickens away. You didn't need to trip me."

The rooster pecked at his nose and squawked loudly.

"Lay off, Gus. I don't need you nipping at this end when I've got whatever it is biting me on the other. Let's get you back into the coop."

After latching the door, Jamie said, "Should I shut the garden gate too?" He was only a little surprised at the responding nudge to his leg. And the growl he heard when he added, "I don't suppose you'd let me pick a few of those raspberries?" didn't surprise him at all. Just to be safe, he picked up the discarded letters to his father. "Who knows what would happen if I littered?" he mumbled.

When at last Jamie turned toward the path, he noticed that the sun had already dropped below the tops of the trees. Black, deeply furrowed clouds were moving down from the north. It did rain less here than in Seattle, but the storms, when they came, were fierce. Jamie hesitated, shifting his weight from leg to leg as he did before a race. Maybe he shouldn't go today. As he looked back at the cabin, he felt something sharp grab his ankle and pull him toward the trail. Jamie winced in pain. "I get it, but if you bite me again I won't be able to walk at all."

He started down the path, surrendering only gradually to the pleasures of the run. His feet slipped into the rhythm of the earth, finding the familiar curves and hillocks of the soft ground. He continued to hear the rough breathing and guttural snorts of his unseen companion, and the smell of wolf mingled with the pine needles he crushed with each footfall.

The smell of wolf! Jamie was a little surprised at how detailed his imaginings were. He'd thought that the wolves were gone, something he'd invented to help him through the difficulties of the past year. Louise was probably right—he'd been alone too much. Still, even if he was inventing it, he was pleased to have the company.

Especially since Louise had disappeared. He admitted to himself that part of the reason he had been so angry with her was because she was right. He should have written to his father. But he was still upset with his dad. It wasn't just the sudden farewell—they hadn't really talked at all since his mother's death. And what about that note? The rows of symbols at the bottom of the page refused to yield their meaning. Why had his father written something Jamie couldn't understand? He knew his dad loved him, but . . . As usual, it seemed to Jamie, Dai-Jeong hadn't bothered to think about him at all.

Responding to a nudge on his leg, Jamie curved through the trees, his attention on his thoughts and not on the trail. After a few such nudges, he realized that it was taking much longer than usual to reach the mountain. Just then, he came out of the trees into a large and unfamiliar clearing. He turned around, hoping to follow his own trail back to a point he recognized. He was beginning to feel light-headed from not eating and, at this point, decided to return to the cabin rather than try to get in a dig. Before he could start back, however, there was a warning snap at his ankle. "Okay, okay—but what's going on?" He was beginning to feel anxious.

The clearing was so regular in circumference that he guessed it was made intentionally. Judging from the thick trunks of the encircling trees, and the lack of any stumps or undergrowth, it had been there a very long time. He relaxed a bit as he saw the mountain rising up not too far away. He could probably find his way back using it as a landmark. Jamie walked slowly toward the sound of running water—no growl, no snap. He wondered if he was alone now, or if he was just doing what the wolf, or what he thought of as a wolf, wanted him to do.

"Are you still here?" Jamie asked. "This is like a movie I wouldn't go see."

Just ahead, a small brook spilled through the trees. Jamie looked down at the stones glistening in the streambed. The hairs stood out on his neck and arms. He knew this place. This was where he'd found the large chunk of quartz. It was years ago, but he was sure of it. On the far bank the gnarled and knotted roots of a stand of willow clawed their way into the running water. Bigger now, but that made sense. Jamie remembered the way his father's fingers had woven willow branches into a shallow basket. Why hadn't anyone told him that he'd been here before? What else had happened that day? Bits and pieces came back to him: his parents laughing with friends, everyone eating lots of food, his pleasure at finding the shimmering stone, someone playing music.

He opened his pack and pulled out the field book. He quickly flipped through the pages, looking for the picture of his family. The photograph fluttered to the ground. Jamie crouched down to pick it up. He'd looked at it for years without really seeing it. Now he studied it closely. He tilted the photo to bring it into focus. It had to be this place. Even in the dim light, the details stood out clearly. He couldn't tell who had taken the picture, but he saw who else was there that day. In the background of the picture, partly hidden by the trees, were two wolves: One was big, black and battered; the other, staring right at the camera, was a golden cub.

The wind whipped around him, and a large drop of rain fell on the photograph. Jamie looked up to check the sky and saw instead a pair of golden eyes the same color as his own—the same color, but far from human. He was nearly nose to nose with the large black wolf. He stood up. "I didn't imagine you. You're real." His throat was constricted with fear.

The wolf took one slow step forward. The storm hit with a ferocity that would have further frightened Jamie had he noticed. He didn't. He had fainted.

A tree snapped and slammed into the earth, something slithered over his ankle. Jamie shuddered but his eyes remained closed. Just below the roar of the storm, he thought he heard a wolf panting, and then flute music. It sounded like the songs he'd heard over and over again from his mother's office in the weeks before she'd died.

"Hungry," Jamie whimpered as he struggled toward consciousness.

The music stopped, and so did the panting. Jamie heard an unfamiliar voice growl, "Why was he so frightened?"

". . . hasn't figured it out yet. Give him time." The words were muffled, but this sounded like Louise.

"No time! If you are to travel with the rest of us this winter, it has to happen soon. I won't leave you here alone again."

"We can't just tell him. He's older now—he has to figure it out himself. He has to believe in order for it to work on him. Remember how difficult it was for you?"

"Never should have left him so long, I don't care what she thought. Start him on the flute now. It doesn't matter if he believes or not. I don't need him to come with us, I just need him to play the music. And hurry—it's going to be a bitter winter."

"I know."

"Louise, is that you?" Jamie struggled to speak clearly. He turned to the voices, forced his eyes open, but saw only a glint of gold before the sounds faded.

The next time Jamie woke, it was dark. What remained of the storm rumbled in the distance. He pushed himself cautiously to his knees, but even so, his feet slipped on the muddy ground. The moon shone through the thinning clouds, and Jamie could make out the edges of the clearing. He heard the stream, gorged with rain now, rushing over its banks. No music, no voices: He must have imagined them. But not the wolf—he was sure he hadn't imagined that. He crawled toward a large tree and maneuvered his stiff body against the trunk, and was reassured by the feel of the rough bark against his back.

After his eyes became comfortable with the subtle light of the moon, and he comfortable with its silvered shadows, Jamie stood and looked around for his belongings. They weren't there. He paced the perimeter of the clearing. Occasionally he poked his foot into the trees at the edges, or kicked at a log or rock that, briefly glimpsed, looked as though it could have been a backpack. The memory of the ragged-looking wolf made him reluctant to leave the open area to search further.

Returning to the safety of the tree, he slouched back down against its base. He thought about the wolves. They had always seemed real to him, but real in the way that his dreams were real. The wolf he'd seen earlier this evening was different. He remembered its warm breath and the drops of saliva congealed on its jaw. Jamie tried to recall if it had seemed vicious, then decided not to think of it at all. He was afraid that if he did, the wolf would show up again. What was

Madame Mahoney's phrase when she quietly walked up behind students whispering in class? *Quand on parle du loup, on en voit la queue.* When one speaks of the wolf, one sees its tail.

He stood and looked, unsuccessfully, for the mountain above the tops of the trees. He studied the position of the moon. No, he thought ruefully, it won't help. I really should have spent less time looking down. He checked over his shoulder and started to run, hoping instinct would guide him. After a few dead ends and switchbacks, his anxiety increased. The darkness seemed to be made of shadows within shadows. He tripped a number of times, stumbling over fallen logs, and once bumped something softer. He kept moving, afraid to stop. Something whipped his face. He screamed and reached up to protect himself. Ready to fight, he lashed out. He was surprised to grab not fur, but fabric. It was the red cloth that marked the trail to Louise's.

Jamie dropped to all fours, struggling to breathe. When he finally looked up, he stared at the incline in disbelief. Heavy rains had eroded the talus. Mud slides and deep gullies had left the areas he had carefully charted and excavated unfamiliar. Jamie was tired and scared. But he was also a skilled observer. He automatically began to note the topographic changes to his work site.

The rain had only recently stopped. As he clambered up the talus, he could still hear faint thunder, and here and there rivulets flowed down the mountain's scarred surface. Still, it was evident that he was not the first one to have climbed here since the storm.

The tracks of some kind of animal crisscrossed the area. Jamie studied the prints left in the mud. A wolf. Maybe two. He bent down to get a closer look in the dim light. Definitely two. One large, the other smaller. There was something else as well, the tracks of a third animal: a barefoot human.

Jamie tried following the tracks, but the prints ended suddenly in a confusion of trampled ground before leading back down the slope. The mud near the point where the trail turned was piled in a soft mound, almost as though something had been buried.

He scuffed at the soil with his toe and uncovered the tip of a cylindrical object. He crouched and, using his fingers, began to brush away the loose soil. Carefully he lifted the object from the ground, blowing the loose dirt from its surface, then held it slightly off to the side, out of his shadow. He tilted it back and forth in the dim light of the moon. Small round holes punctured its length, and numerous delicate carvings were etched onto the surface. One end was broader than the other, flaring slightly, and a large chip was missing from the tip. Jamie knew what it was right away. "A bone flute," he whispered. His mother had spoken of these and their importance to her research. She had had a photograph of one pinned to her office wall. He tried to remember what she had said they were used for.

Without thinking, he brought the flute to his lips and blew. Immediately he heard three things: a clear sweet tone that made him long for his home and family, a woman's voice that shouted "No!" and the sound of thousands of tons of rocks and mud rushing toward him. Jamie dropped the flute and desperately tried to find a purchase on the slippery ground. Unable to get out of the way, he flung himself behind a fallen tree moments before the rocks crashed down on him.

"Jamie! Jamie, wake up."

The voice sounded dull. At first he thought it was coming from a great distance, but then he felt a hand on his shoulder, gently shaking him. "I'm awake. Stop poking me." After a long pause, he added, "Louise? Is that you?"

"Yes. Don't move."

Jamie opened his eyes. She had to be kidding. It was not yet dawn, but there was enough light for him to make out his left leg. It was twisted at an odd angle, pinned between the fallen tree and a large boulder. Smaller pieces of scree and rubble were piled on his chest, making it hard to breathe. Something warm oozed down his cheek.

"Move? Don't worry. I won't," he replied. He hurt all over.

"It will take me some time to dig you out. And I can pull you back to the cabin on a travois made of branches. Do you know what that is?"

"Louise, later," Jamie whispered. "I know I'll love hearing

all about it. But not now."

"Jamie." She looked at him for a moment, then opened the small leather pouch that she always wore. "Can you swallow? I want you to take these herbs. I . . . They're strong Jamie, for the pain; they'll make you sleep."

"My leg's not really that bad. Most of the weight of the rock seems to be on the tree. I'm hungry, though. Do you have anything to eat?"

"Teenagers!" The forced humor did not quite mask the worry in her voice. "Try these."

She placed a small amount of the dried herbs in his mouth.

Jamie chewed the bitter leaves. "Yuck. Are these from the garden? I should have pulled them out when I had the chance." He struggled to stay awake. "I found a flute . . . " he mumbled as he drifted off.

"I need help," Louise cried.

Jamie thought he saw two shadows leave the cover of the trees. "Careful," he heard his aunt say. "Please be careful."

He blacked out again as the wolves began to dig him free.

Mulberry

CHAPTER 5

DEAR JAMIE,
DON'T MOVE. OR ELSE.
I'LL BE BACK.
LOUISE

Louise had written the note in big block letters and propped it on the table. Jamie could read it easily from where he lay on her bed. "Or else?" What else could she to do? It seemed to him as though nothing more could possibly happen.

Fragmented scenes from the previous night floated through his thoughts like leaves in the storm-swollen creek. He was unable to piece together anything coherent. And what he did remember seemed unlikely: He thought he'd seen Louise standing in the doorway of the cabin talking to someone. At one point she sighed and leaned against the doorframe and Jamie could see beyond her to the front steps. A large black wolf stared into the cabin, turned, and loped away. Louise watched it go, then stepped out the door into the clearing.

"Must have been dreaming," Jamie mumbled. Then he moaned, pulled a bright pink-and-yellow quilt over his head, and went back to sleep.

Sometime later, the smell of coffee and the unmistakable squeal of the hinges on the chicken-coop door roused him. He rolled over and let out a squeal of his own. His left leg felt as though it had been crushed by a rock. And then he remembered—it had. So it hadn't been a dream. But the wolves? He was sure he'd seen the one in the clearing. Everything else seemed a bit unreal—that is, everything except for the hollow ache in his stomach. He eyed a platter of biscuits placed in the middle of the table.

He carefully rolled to the side of the bed and stood, keeping his head low out of habit. He winced a bit but was pleasantly surprised to find that he could put weight on his leg. "Not broken then," he muttered. He hopped toward the table and slid into the nearest chair. He swallowed the first four biscuits whole, chewed the next three, and by the time he was on the eighth had begun to feel more human.

"Human!" He snorted at the absurdity of this thought,

given the variety of companions he'd had over the past twenty-four hours. What was real? What had he imagined? He grabbed another biscuit and leaned way back in his chair and chewed. A bit stale, he thought. I wonder if they're the same ones I tried to take yesterday.

"Put all four legs of that chair back on the floor. Do you want to tip? You might hurt yourself," Louise barked as she came inside.

He stared at her in disbelief. Yesterday she had left him without food, abandoned him in an electrical storm, and given him herbs that knocked him out—and now she was concerned for his safety? Still, he didn't want to make her angry; he wanted to talk about what had happened. "Good morning," he responded politely. He shifted his weight and the chair dropped forward.

She plopped the basket she carried onto the table with such force that a small sage-green egg bounced out, rolled across the table, and smashed onto the floor. "Didn't you see my note? I told you not to move." She glared at him, but he noticed the corners of her mouth twitched a bit as she reached for the last biscuit and sat down. "How did you sleep?"

"Weird dreams. How did I get back here?"

Louise chewed vigorously, not bothering to answer. She took a long time to finish the biscuit. Finally she brushed the crumbs from her hands, stood up, and strode toward the doorway.

"Louise!" he shouted. He couldn't believe she would leave without talking to him.

She stopped, then sighed in resignation. "All right, we'll talk." She turned back to him. "But let me clean up the egg."

Jamie watched her as she moved around the cabin. When she had put the kettle on the stove and added a few small logs to the fire, he relaxed a bit and slouched in his chair. It was unlikely that she'd leave a cup of hot coffee. He banged his leg as he shifted position, not quite stifling the automatic yelp.

Louise swallowed and closed her eyes for a moment. But when she spoke, her voice was normal. "No chores today."

"Probably not, but I do need to get outside."

Hobbling across the clearing was more difficult than he had expected. About halfway to the outhouse, he studied the remaining distance and the high step up into the privy, decided it was too much, and settled instead for turning back to the small stand of hawthorn he had just passed.

Louise raised her eyebrows when he returned and eased himself back into a chair. "Faster than I thought you'd be," she said, but made no other comment. She was at the counter, using a large mortar and pestle. "Arnica," she announced a few minutes later. She used the fingers of her right hand to scrape the dark-green paste into her left palm. Then she started to walk toward him. He must have looked horrified, because she quickly said, "No, you don't need to eat it—it's medicine for your leg." He eyed her skeptically as she spread it on his bruises. The teakettle began to whistle. Louise wiped her hands and jumped up to make the coffee.

"Now then," she said when it was done, "how about a cup?" She sat down, filled a large mug, and pushed it toward him. When he shook his head and began to slide it back to her, she held up her hand and said, "No, take it. You don't have to drink any, but I think you'll want the hot cup in your hands before we're done."

Jamie sighed in exasperation but took the cup; he didn't want to put her off now. Somewhat to his surprise, he immediately realized she was right. The heat and weight and rough surface of the mug were real and comforting. Holding a coffee cup was normal, Jamie thought, a normal thing that normal people do—quite a contrast to the strangeness of the preceding day.

He looked at his aunt. She sipped her coffee. She stared out a window. Took off her glasses and then put them back on. Began to hum. Clearly she thought that if he wanted to talk, it was his responsibility to get the conversation going. He clutched the mug between his shaky hands and wondered what to say first. "I saw a wolf here yesterday."

"You knew there were wolves here. I wouldn't have left you alone if they were dangerous."

"Where were you?"

"I went for supplies." She looked into her cup.

"How did you dig me out last night?"

"I had help," she said at last. "I've mentioned the neighbors—I called for them."

Jamie eyed her suspiciously. Even when she answered his questions, he didn't get the information he wanted. "Why were you there when it happened?"

"I came home at dinnertime and you weren't here. Figured you'd holed up somewhere during the storm. But then, when you didn't come back, I thought I had better go and look for you. When I got to the mountain, the stones were already rumbling. I looked up and saw you bent down over something. I shouted at you, but, well . . ." Louise shrugged. "You seemed pretty absorbed in what you were doing. I heard it—the flute. There wasn't enough time to get to you." She shrugged again and searched his face. "It did make me think you might like this, though. Something to do while your leg heals. I don't think you'll be running for a while." Her face was serious as she pulled something out of her pocket and laid it on the table.

Jamie flinched. It was another flute. Not the one he'd found on the mountain—that had been caked with dirt, darkened with age, and broken at the tip. No, this was newer, but similar. It too seemed to be made of bone, with the same strange carvings around the finger holes. Jamie reached out to touch it, then quickly pulled back as he remembered the rock slide.

"Coincidence."

"What?" he said.

"The rock slide, a coincidence. It just happened to occur at the same time you blew the flute. I picked up that one for you." She pulled out the broken flute and pushed it toward him.

Jamie's fingers twitched. He longed to pick up the flutes, but something held him back. "Tell me about them," he said warily. "Where do they come from?" That single remembered note haunted him; it might not have caused the rock slide, but it was powerful all the same.

Louise cocked her head, trying to gauge his mood. "Here. They come from here. I'm surprised you haven't found any in your digging before this. They turn up fairly frequently." She reached out and picked up the newer flute. "This is a nice example. It's a bit more recent than most of the others and in excellent condition. See? No cracks, and the designs are quite clear." The expression in her eyes softened as she cradled it in her hands. "It's a lovely thing, isn't it?"

She held it out to him, but he shook his head. She placed it back on the table and continued talking. "Your mother—we've hardly spoken of her, have we?" Louise looked up as he twisted uncomfortably in his chair. "She was always fascinated by these—we used to play together, before . . . Anyway, she asked me to send her one last fall. I was reluctant to have it leave the mountain; the flutes seem to belong here. But you know how your mother loved music. She said she was going to give it to you, that she would teach you to play, so I sent it. I don't think she did, did she?"

"No," Jamie whispered, unsure of what else to say, remembering the eerie melodies he'd heard from his mother's study all last fall.

"I wanted you to learn the flute—wanted to have you come before—but she wouldn't allow it. Well, this one's yours now. A gift. I'm going out to the garden. I'll make us some lunch in a bit." She stood up and took a sip of the now-cold coffee before she walked toward the door. "Take it easy on the leg," she called, heading out into the clearing.

Jamie put his hands on the table and looked at the flute. He picked it up and rolled it between the palms of his hands. "Okay," he said out loud. "Here goes nothing." He lifted it to his lips and blew softly. The whistle squeaked. He blew again. It screeched—but the ground beneath his feet remained steady, the plates stayed on the shelves. Jamie took a deep breath. Covering the small holes one by one, he explored the sounds of the flute. The tones climbed steadily and Jamie's heart soared; he had the oddest feeling, as though something he had once lost had been returned to him.

Jamie examined the flute. He mirrored the careful way Louise had cradled it in her hands. He stroked its surface. Five holes. He slid his thumb down the row, pausing briefly to cover each opening in turn, then traced the delicate carvings. There must be at least a hundred of them, and they were familiar somehow. He bent his head close to the table, tilting the flute so it caught the rays of the morning sun. Not pictures, he thought, but not merely decorative either. The geometrical marks were arranged in long rows, almost like writing, but it wasn't an alphabet he recognized. Jamie sat up suddenly. They were like the marks on the bottom of his father's letter. He tried to stand up and was surprised at the quick shock of pain. At that moment Louise returned from the garden. She rushed to his side.

"Jamie! What is it? Are you all right?" Her face tightened with worry as she put her arms around him.

"My backpack! I need something from my backpack!"

"It's okay. Sit down—let me check your leg."

"I need to get my pack. I lost it last night." He broke from her hold and moved toward the door, taking a few strides before he fell.

"Jamie, stop! You'll damage your leg. I'll find the pack."

Louise stepped over him on her way out of the cabin. She neither looked down nor made any effort to help him up. He struggled to his knees and, supporting his weight on his elbows, watched her leave. Rather than head for the trail, though, she turned and walked behind the cabin, quickly returning with the backpack bundled in her arms.

She held herself oddly, Jamie thought, as though she were trying to avoid eye contact with someone hidden in the low shrubbery at the edge of the clearing. He glanced in that direction but didn't see anything.

"That was fast," said Jamie with some asperity as she came back inside. He struggled to stand, but there was nothing to grab, so he ended up crawling to the table before pulling himself upright.

"Well, yes, it was."

"You had it all along. Where did you find it? Why didn't you give it to me sooner?"

Louise dropped the pack next to the coffee cups and eyed him with a mixture of concern and impatience. "You didn't ask. And I didn't want to upset you," she said at last. "It got quite wet." Without another word, she turned and headed back to the garden.

Jamie sat down and reached for the pack. He struggled a bit with the zipper, finally using a spoon to chip off the dried mud that prevented it from moving. The corner of his field book was instantly visible, but when Jamie pulled it out, his initial relief changed to despair. The cover was warped and soggy; his careful records, the results of weeks of work, were barely legible. He flipped through the pages looking for the note from his father. It wasn't there.

He dumped the contents of the pack on the table, searching for the letter. Then he paged through the notebook again. He didn't find the note, but there was the old photograph. He remembered holding it as the storm hit. How had it gotten back into the pack? He carefully peeled it from the page and examined it, rubbing the spots left by the rain. It wasn't too damaged. Someone must have picked this up right away, he thought, turning the picture over. On the back of the photo was part of a muddy paw print.

Jamie looked up at a noise from the doorway.

"Okay?" asked Louise.

"A letter is missing."

She shrugged. "It was very windy."

"I need to find it."

"I'll look later. But not now." She turned away from him. "How about some lunch?"

While Louise cooked, Jamie limped to the thicket of hawthorn, then to the pump. I'll write to my dad, he thought as he splashed the cold water on his face. I'll ask him to send the marks again. He returned to the cabin just as Louise was placing the food on the table. "Smoked trout, the last of it," she said with a theatrical sigh. "I'll have to teach you how to make it. After you learn the flute, that is."

"I'm not *that* hungry." Jamie wrinkled his nose.

"I don't know why you don't like it—especially since you enjoy fresh trout so much. Well . . ." She shrugged and put the plate down anyway.

"It's all yours. But I would like to learn to play." He reached over the trout to pick up the flute.

"No, eat. You have to keep up your strength. This will be hard work, and we don't have long."

Jamie thought she must be joking, but she was looking out the window, judging the angle of the sun with a serious look on her face.

"I think we have just a little time to talk."

Jamie continued to hold the flute in his right hand while trying to scrape the skin off the trout with his left. "Why is it so important to start right now?"

Louise watched his awkward movements. "You could use both hands."

Jamie grinned but didn't let go of the flute. He shoved a bite into his mouth.

"It can take quite a while to master. And I'd like you to learn enough here to play on your own when you get back to Seattle. I'm glad you like it."

Jamie, his mouth full, shook his head and grimaced.

"Not the trout. The flute. Your father will be pleased."

Still chewing, he raised his eyebrows in question.

"Did you know he has written a number of papers discussing their significance? He calls them wolf whistles. He thinks human hunters used them to call forth the strength of the wolves. Or, maybe, to actually call forth wolves."

Jamie choked on a bone.

Louise continued as though she didn't notice. "I'll not say that he's wrong, although other scholars view them differently." She stopped to eat a radish. "Your father started studying the flutes when he was a doctoral student. He thinks . . .

Well, anyway, I have some of the articles. I'll give them to you. He believes the flutes were first brought here from Mongolia over the Bering Land Bridge. He used to come here with your mother to dig for them. They met at college, you know."

Jamie nodded.

"Sometimes they would bring friends. It was fun to have company." Her voice faded, and she stared out the window for a moment before continuing. "After they were married and you were born, they kept coming for a while. Those were happy times. You loved it here." She smiled at Jamie. "But then your mother . . ." Louise stood and began to clear the dishes.

Abruptly she sat back down again and reached for his arm. "When she got sick . . . Did you know she'd been sick for a number of years?"

Jamie shook his head.

"No. I thought not. Well, it doesn't matter now." She paused. "When she got sick, she didn't want to bring you any-more. She was afraid of what she couldn't understand, afraid you wouldn't want to go back home with her, I think." Louise looked at him. "It hurt me, but I couldn't fault her, for she did love you, Jamie—more than anything. But now we must make up for lost time." Her voice was grim.

Jamie's jaw hung open slightly; he had finished chewing but still didn't speak.

Louise looked at him; her teeth gleamed in the late afternoon sun. "Close your mouth. It's not that bad. It's okay, trust me."

Trust Louise. He looked at her teeth. *Trust Louise.* That's what his father had said.

"No, again. Try it again."

The sun had dropped below the tops of the pines. The cabin had begun to grow dark, although a few shafts of dust-filled light still flowed between the trunks of the trees and across the clearing. Jamie brought the flute back to his lips. He had started the day tired and sore; by now, exhaustion had drawn the color from his face and left shadows under his eyes. Louise looked at him and sighed. "Try it again, but not right now. Why don't you go outside for a bit while there's still light?"

Jamie looked at her. He was almost too tired to move, but she was right. Once it got dark, he would have a lot more trouble getting around. He didn't want to fall on his leg. He rose stiffly and pushed himself up from the table with one arm. He started toward the doorway with the flute in his hand.

"Jamie, leave the flute here. You'll need both hands to, uh, work the pump."

Jamie looked down at his shoes and grinned a little sheepishly. "You know," he said, "it's crazy, but I don't want to put it down. It's almost as though it's part of me." He shrugged and looked up at his aunt and noticed something different in her expression. Respect, he thought. She's looking at me as though I'm a grown-up—the way the coach looks when I've run a really good race.

Louise handed him one of her sweaters. "Here, it's cold. Be careful on the step."

Jamie drew a sharp breath that hissed between his clenched teeth as he eased himself out of the cabin. Even with most of his weight braced against the doorjamb, he was surprised at how much he hurt. Maneuvering outside on the flat ground was better, although limping was uncomfortable no matter how he favored the injured leg. Finally he settled on a kind of low hop as the best method of moving forward, his arms outstretched for balance, the flute still in his hand, Louise's sweater flapping in the breeze. Good thing no one is watching me, he thought. I must look ridiculous.

As he approached the grove of hawthorn, there was a slight rustling. He was being watched after all. Two wolves emerged from the trees at the far edge of the clearing. One was large, black, and—familiar. The other, smaller and golden furred, crouched in the shadows. Despite Louise's assurances that the wolves would not attack, Jamie instinctively raised his hand to his face to protect himself. The flute brushed against his lips as he did so. Without thinking, he did what he'd been doing all evening: He blew. A single note echoed through the clearing. The smaller of the two wolves stood. A second note. The young wolf began to trot toward him.

Jamie blew a third note, so sharp and shrill it seemed to rip the air within the glade. The advancing wolf stopped and tipped its head. Jamie brought the flute back to his lips. But he was trembling now, too nervous to breathe, let alone play. The larger wolf stepped out of the trees, steering its smaller companion back into the woods. It was quickly becoming dark, but even in the shadows Jamie could see the black wolf's gaze linger on him for a long moment. Its eyes held a look of respect remarkably like the one that Louise had just given him.

"Back so soon? I thought you'd take a longer break," said Louise, as he hobbled to the table.

"There are wolves outside."

"I've known them to listen to the flutes. Do they worry you?"

"No. I guess not. You seem sure they won't hurt me."

"They won't," said his aunt. "Can we keep practicing?"

They continued to work for hours. The candles Louise had lit at dusk burned out and were replaced by a second set; the fire in the woodstove had also burned low, and the room was chilly. Jamie pulled Louise's sweater close and looked out the window.

"Try it again, Jamie. You almost have it."

He'd been struggling with a complicated series of tones.

"No, that's not right. Faster in the middle. And a little softer at the end. Try again."

"I'm too tired." He was, in fact, so exhausted, he could barely suck in the breath he needed to play. "Why is it so important?"

"I'm going to invite the neighbors to hear you play."

He started to protest, but one look at Louise silenced his complaints. She looked slightly wild, and her eyes burned in the dim room. They worked for another hour.

"That's it," she cried at last. "Oh Jamie, you've done it."

He put the flute down with great relief and tried to stand.

"Where do you think you're going? We're not done yet." She glanced at the door, then reached into her pouch and pulled out another flute. "Now try it with me. What I play won't sound like your melody. Just hold on to your own notes, okay? It's important to get it right."

Jamie watched her raise the flute. It was a bit longer than his, the elegant designs carved into the bone a bit more numerous. She caught his gaze and held it. Slowly, carefully, Jamie ran though the sequence. His notes sometimes matched Louise's, sometimes harmonized. More often they created a compelling, if unusual, dissonance.

They finished at the same time, lowering their flutes simultaneously, still looking at each other. "Good work." Jamie saw Louise mouth the words, but the sound of her voice was muffled by loud thumps on the door.

He was breathless after playing for so long. The unexpected knocking made him gasp. Louise smiled at him reassuringly and stood up. She turned to the door as a loud whack forced it open.

He saw two people framed in the narrow opening: a girl, and a man who stood behind her, his hands resting gently on her shoulders. The man seemed familiar. Jamie looked at Louise out of the corner of his eye. He tried to gauge her re-action to the unannounced visitors. Were these the neighbors she had mentioned?

She strode toward them, tipping over a chair and a basket of cherries in her enthusiasm. She embraced each of them, her smile and her arms lingering on the man a moment longer. She pulled them into the cabin and said, "Jamie, this is, umm . . . my goddaughter. That's right, my goddaughter, Cicely."

Jamie saw the girl's eyes crinkle in amusement. She was about his age, with unusual coloring: dark golden hair and skin, golden eyes, very white teeth. He looked away from her with some reluctance as Louise proceeded with the introduc-tions.

"And this . . ." She gestured toward the man, then paused and flapped her hand. She seemed unusually flustered. Cicely grinned. Louise took a breath and continued quickly. "This is Ji-Min." The man's forbidding expression was lightened by a twitch of humor at the corners of his mouth. Cicely giggled and then bent her head as Louise gave her a stern look.

Jamie looked at the man. He wasn't tall but was solid and

muscular, with broad shoulders and skin the color of dark honey. His long black hair was pulled back in a leather thong. A streak of gray made Jamie think he might be a bit older than he looked. Probably older than Dai-Jeong. Dad, thought Jamie, staring as the man picked up the scattered fruit. That's who he reminds me of. He looks like my dad.

Louise was still talking, repeating something Jamie hadn't responded to. "Jamie, Ji-Min is my husband. He's brought Cicely here to stay with us for a while. Jamie?"

The man had finished gathering the cherries. As he gracefully rose, basket in hand, he caught Jamie's look and smiled. Jamie couldn't picture his dad in a flannel shirt, let alone a ponytail, but take off his father's glasses and, yes, the resemblance was remarkable. He opened his mouth to speak and then closed it, unable to think of what to say.

The man reached out and stroked Jamie's cheek, then affectionately rumpled his hair. With a very faint Korean accent he said, "Ji-Min. My name is Ji-Min, a bit like yours, but Korean. Did Louise give you your pack? I found it in the woods last night. Picked up some papers and a photo, too. Hope you can salvage them."

Jamie stared.

"We heard you playing the flute as we came to the door. Are you a beginner? You play well." He watched, not without sympathy, as Jamie struggled unsuccessfully to respond. Then, after nodding once, Ji-Min turned away and put the basket back on the table. Grabbing Louise roughly by the waist, he pulled her close and whispered something. She smiled, then nodded. He walked out into the darkness through the still-open door.

Jamie finally found his voice. "Your husband?"

"Why yes, of course." Louise bent to pick up the chair. "Do you think you can climb the ladder? It's time for bed."

"But . . ."

"Good night."

Nasturtium

CHAPTER 6

Hello.
Louise and I have gone for supplies.
Please milk my goats.
Your friend, Cicely

Jamie saw the note as he climbed down from the loft. He jumped, landing on his good leg. It had been nearly two weeks since the rock slide. His injuries had responded well to his aunt's mix of herbs, massage, and impatience. The swelling was gone, and the bruises were faded to the color of overripe peaches. He was more than ready to start running, but Louise kept a hawk's watch on him. Now, savoring his freedom, he climbed up the ladder and jumped again.

Jamie had known they were going; Louise had told him the night before. He'd already promised Cicely—two or three times—that he'd take care of her beloved goats. Either she had been afraid he'd forget or Louise had suggested the note as a way to make Cicely practice her writing. Jamie picked up the paper and grinned. Louise was right—Cicely did need to practice. He traced the awkward letters, his smile deepening as he came to the final words: "Your friend." The girl fit so easily into the rhythms of this place that Jamie could not now imagine life here without her. He too felt he'd found a friend.

He picked up one of the slightly burned pancakes stacked on the table, took a bite, and gagged as a large lump of bak-ing soda dissolved on his tongue. Cicely must have made breakfast. A friend, but not a cook. Even Louise did better. He took a sip of cold coffee and gagged again. They're lucky I've been preparing the meals, he thought. Maybe that's why Louise won't let me leave the clearing.

He had not really minded, though. In fact, if he was being honest with himself, he'd have to admit that he had enjoyed the past few weeks very much. Far from being bored, he was completely content to hang around with Cicely. She slept downstairs on a mat spread out near the woodstove, and when he woke each day, he would lie in bed and listen for her before coming down. She was a more lively breakfast companion than his aunt.

"Your goddaughter? Where are her parents?" Jamie had asked the first morning after her arrival.

"Not here. She's been staying with Ji-Min." Louise whispered her response. "Let's not wake her by talking—she'll be tired."

He'd asked again, many times, but little had ever been said to fully explain her sudden appearance. Cicely was nearly as good as his aunt at dodging questions. Unlike his aunt, though, she asked hundreds of her own, and she was always ready to listen to the details of his life in Seattle.

Mornings were spent, as they had been before the accident, doing chores. Cicely helped him when she finished milking her goats, Daisy and Violet. After lunch, they had a bit of free time when they would talk or play with another one of Cicely's "pets," a large, vocal raven.

"Jamie, this is my friend Ace," she announced the first time the bird had swooped into the clearing.

"Ace? Did you name him? Why isn't he named after a plant, like you and the goats?"

Cicely rolled her eyes. She tossed a pebble into the air. Ace flapped his wings and soared into the air. Jamie watched as the bird caught the small rock in his beak and dropped it in Cicely's outstretched hand. They repeated this three more times, each toss higher than the preceding one. Then Cicely turned to Jamie and said, "His name is Ace. He's also good at tag."

Late each afternoon Louise would call them in for the "lessons," a period of a couple hours during which his aunt, unusually stern faced and officious, would sit Cicely down with a pen, some paper, and a writing assignment, while Jamie played the bone flute. If either one of them stopped for more than a few seconds, Louise would look up from the books she was reading and glare in their direction, the fierce gaze magnified by her eyeglasses. Jamie loved the flute and was happy to practice, but her insistence seemed a bit extreme to him.

"She's worse than Madame Mahoney," Jamie whispered one afternoon when Louise had gone to get water.

"What?"

"Madame Mahoney. My French teacher. She's strict, but not as bad as Louise."

"Oh," replied Cicely, although she still looked confused.

"*Parlez-vous français?*" asked Jamie. Receiving no response, he added, "What foreign language do you study in school?"

"School?" Cicely seemed perplexed. "English, I guess." She squirmed in her chair.

He looked up to see his aunt standing in the doorway and wondered, somewhat sheepishly, how much of the conversation she'd overheard. Coming into the cabin, she tripped, and the bucket of water she was carrying spilled all over the floor. It was only later, after they'd cleaned up the mess, that he realized she had, intentionally or not, successfully kept him from asking any further questions. Was she trying to keep something from him? Or just protecting Cicely?

Now, as Jamie fingered Cicely's note, he remembered the confused look on her face that day. It was odd. She seemed to have no reference point for his discussions about school, and clearly had great difficulty writing and spelling, yet she seemed so intelligent. Dinner conversations, for example, lively before she came, were now almost too fast for him to follow. Cicely was passionate and articulate, holding her own against Louise in a way that Jamie never could. Night after night she peppered Louise with questions: What herbs did you use in this stew? How did you braid your hair like that? Why are you reading that book? When are we going to the market? Her voice was a bit higher than Louise's, but with the same smoky, almost rough quality. Jamie loved to watch his persistent friend pursue his elusive aunt. The varying pitch of their voices, and the tilt of their heads, communicated almost as much as their words.

Out in the clearing, Gus crowed and the goats started to bray. Jamie pocketed Cicely's note and stepped outside, surprised by how high the sun was. No wonder the animals are restless, he thought. It's late. After using the outhouse, he paused briefly at the goat pen but decided to gather eggs first. This proved to be a lapse of judgment that Jamie would not soon forget. By the time he got to the goats, they were feisty, butting their heads against the side of the pen and pawing the ground. They little resembled the docile pets that followed Cicely around.

Jamie reached for the gate and one of the goats stared at him. Her eyes glinted with what he took to be malevolence. "Hey, Daisy, how's it going?"

The goat curled her lip, exposing large yellow teeth.

"Okay then, maybe you're Violet." Jamie had not learned to tell the two goats apart, although Cicely had cataloged their differences for him more than once. To him, they both looked exactly the same: brown and scruffy. He undid the latch and slipped into the pen. Their food bins and water trough were empty. "I know how it goes," he said. "I'm hungry too." This attempt at companionable banter was apparently not very convincing: Yellow-tooth grabbed his shirt and started chewing. Jamie pulled free and picked up the pail Cicely used for milking. "I think I'll start with your buddy," he said, edging away from the goat. She still had a bit of T-shirt protruding from her mouth.

He turned to the second goat. Her normally white beard was stained blue from the berries Cicely had hand-fed her yesterday. "Violet?"

She hissed.

"Daisy, then."

The goat lowered her head and began to run at Jamie. He scooted out of her path. "Don't get so huffy—I'll learn your names, I promise."

Gus had sauntered over to the pen and was crowing loudly.

"I don't need your advice," Jamie snapped at him. "It's not

my fault they're too ugly to tell apart. What does Cicely see in them?"

Now both goats glared at him.

"Maybe you just need something to eat," he said, putting down the bucket. "How about some pancakes? I'll go and get them."

Jamie noticed that the goats weren't looking him in the eye anymore. They'd fixed their gaze at his waist, or maybe a bit lower. They began to charge. He quickly picked up the milk bucket and held it in front of himself.

The pail twanged loudly as they hit, and his arms throbbed, but the makeshift shield had done its job.

He tried to scramble over the fence, but Yellow-tooth grabbed his shirt again.

"That's not very nice," he cried, struggling to pull free.

Meanwhile, Bluebeard edged behind him and started to squeeze through the gate.

"Oh, no you don't," Jamie shouted, attempting to disentangle himself from the now shredded T-shirt.

Gus, seeing his friend in trouble, decided to help. He darted over to the escaping goat and pecked at her forelegs. She stopped short and reared.

Yellow-tooth abruptly let go, and Jamie, unexpectedly freed, lunged forward. He tripped over Bluebeard and landed facedown on the ground, eye to eye with Gus. "We've got to stop meeting like this," he said to the rooster.

Gus bent down and nipped his nose before strutting back to the henhouse.

Bluebeard leaped over Jamie, quickly crossed the clearing, and ran into the woods. He pulled himself to his knees and was trying to stand when he was knocked flat by the hind legs of Yellow-tooth, who headed in the opposite direction.

"Great," said Jamie, spitting out a mouthful of dust. "What else could go wrong?"

In answer, he heard a deep laugh echo across the clearing.

Ji-Min. Jamie groaned and put his head back down. He had not seen Louise's husband since the night of Cicely's arrival. He'd been curious about him, but despite Jamie's many questions, his aunt had given little information. "Ask him yourself," was her usual response. Jamie had longed to do that, and had often imagined chance meetings with Ji-Min. In these daydreams they would sit and talk, in a way that Jamie and his father never had. Their lengthy conversations would include numerous instances of witty comments and profound insights on Jamie's part. (In other versions of this reverie, they would be running together, Jamie easily keeping pace with the athletic-looking Ji-Min.) Not once had Jamie envisioned himself flat on his face, bested by two goats and an old rooster. He groaned again.

Ji-Min crossed the clearing and reached a hand down to help Jamie stand. He scrambled to his feet without the offered help, although his bad leg throbbed. When he stumbled slightly, Ji-Min reached out both arms and caught him by the shoulders.

"Okay?" he asked kindly.

Jamie looked at him. The corners of the man's mouth curled with mirth, but his gaze was concerned. "Yeah, I'm okay, I guess," he said. He looked down and made a show of brushing dirt off his clothes. "A bit embarrassed, though." Jamie felt his face flush.

"Those goats. If you only knew how much trouble they've caused. They're not the best pets for our kind. But Cicely loves them. I call them 'Vile' and 'Crazy'—not that I've ever been able to tell them apart."

Jamie looked up in amazement. Ji-Min seemed like the kind of person who wouldn't be troubled by anything.

"I guess we'd better get them back, though. Cicely would never forgive us if they were lost."

Jamie hesitated before admitting, "I don't know if I can chase after them. My leg hurts too much."

"Don't worry. If you run after them, they just run faster. I finally made Cicely train them to respond to a whistle." He had a leather pouch like Louise's tied to his waist, and after rummaging around for a moment, he pulled something from it. Jamie was startled to see that it was a bone flute, a little shorter and a bit wider in circumference than the one Louise had given him, but with the same type of incised markings around the holes. "They'll think it's Cicely." Bringing the flute to his lips, he played a series of high, crisp notes.

Sure enough, after a moment the two goats peered through the trees, then trotted back into the clearing. Continuing to play, Ji-Min walked into the pen, followed by the now co-operative Daisy and Violet. He quickly slipped out, closing the gate behind him. "That was the easy part. Now we have to figure out how to milk them."

After rejecting a number of plans, and stalling as long as possible, they approached the pen together. Jamie carried a basket of carrots. Ji-Min was armed with the bucket. They unlatched the gate and marched inside, grim faced but res-olute. The goats, though, put up surprisingly little resistance. Either they had tired of torturing Jamie, or they were too hun-gry to bother.

Ji-Min crouched down and started milking the first goat. "You said your leg hurt. How is it now?" he asked without looking up.

"Uh, okay, I guess." Jamie watched the man's back, again noting the resemblance to his father.

"Louise wanted me to stop by and check on you. She was afraid you would try to run and reinjure it."

"Yeah, well . . . I hadn't counted on tripping over a goat, or I might have."

Ji-Min laughed. After a moment he said, "I love to run. I loved it even when I was a boy."

Though Louise had said almost nothing about Ji-Min,

Jamie had drawn his own conclusions. "Did you run with my father?"

"No." There was a bit of sadness in his voice, and his accent seemed more pronounced as he continued. "No. We were very close. But my brother was just a small child when I traveled to this place."

"You *are* my uncle, then?" Jamie was excited. "You're my father's brother?"

Ji-Min nodded.

"Then Louise really is my aunt." Jamie sounded amazed. "She didn't lie."

"She doesn't like to answer questions, but she never lies. Yes, I am your father's brother and her husband."

"You're not around much. Are you separated or something?" Jamie hoped he hadn't gone too far.

Ji-Min stood up and moved over to the second goat. He looked like he might be trying not to smile. "No, I'm crazy about Louise. Couldn't imagine life without her. It's just that I'm not much for being indoors." He paused briefly, as though searching for the right way to say something. "And I do a lot of my work in the evenings." He looked at Jamie and waited for a response.

Jamie wasn't really listening. He was too overwhelmed to do more than stare at the ground and mumble, "I have an uncle and I have an aunt." He repeated this a couple of times, getting used to the sound of it. Suddenly he looked up and asked, "Do I have . . . I mean, do you . . . ?"

"No. Well, there's Cicely—we've cared for her since she was young." Ji-Min stood up and brushed his hands on his shirt. "All done. That went pretty well, I'd say."

Jamie was about to agree when the goat he'd been feeding bit his hand. "Yeoww!"

"What's wro—" The second goat butted Ji-Min from behind before he could finish his question. Grabbing for the milk bucket, he tripped, as one of the now-hostile animals used her head to toss the full pail into the air. The contents sprayed over Jamie before the bucket clanged to the ground.

"Well," said Ji-Min, lying on the ground laughing, "at least you don't need to wash your shirt. There's not enough of it left to be worth saving." He got to his feet and clapped his nephew on the shoulder. "Come on, I'll make us something to eat while you change, and then we'll figure out what to tell Cicely."

They sat on the steps of the cabin, leaning back slightly to catch the warmth of the afternoon sun, their legs stretched out in front of them. Jamie reached for another hot pepper-and-scallion pancake.

"You eat like a wolf," said Ji-Min.

"My dad says that too." He took a large bite.

"It's a Korean recipe," his uncle continued.

"I know," said Jamie swallowing. "Pa jon. My dad makes them."

"Does he?" Ji-Min's voice was quiet. "Did your father ever speak of me?"

Jamie shook his head and took another pancake.

"It has been a long time since I've seen him. Not since you were little."

Jamie grabbed the last pancake. "Did you see me when I came here with my parents?"

"Yes." His uncle stood abruptly, took the empty platter to the pump, and rinsed it. He shook the droplets of water from it, tilted his head to the sky, sniffed.

Jamie felt a shiver run down his back as he watched.

"Does Dai-Jeong know you are learning the flute?" Ji-Min sat back down next to Jamie. His voice had lost some of its warmth.

"What?" said Jamie, suddenly apprehensive.

"Your father. Is he happy you are learning to play the whistle?" Ji-Min reached into the pouch, pulled out his own flute, and handed it to his nephew.

Jamie took it reluctantly. He held it with the tips of his fingers.

His uncle watched him closely. "It's hard work, and Louise is a tough teacher, I bet."

Jamie smiled at this, although he still grasped the flute tentatively, as though it might bite.

"Would you like to try it?"

Jamie shook his head and handed the flute back to his uncle.

"Would you play something for me on your own instrument? I would like to hear how you are progressing."

Jamie shook his head again, suddenly shy. "No, maybe later." He looked up at his uncle, hoping that he hadn't displeased him.

His uncle's gaze did not waver. He searched Jamie's face for a long moment and then nodded. "Okay, but I will ask again. It is important that you learn to play well."

"Why?"

"What has Louise told you about these?" Ji-Min slipped the bone whistle back into his pouch.

"Not much. That not many people know about these instruments. That fewer people know how to play them. Why?"

"Have you not wondered why she has pushed you so hard?"

Jamie shrugged. "I asked. She said I had to learn to play them before the end of the summer. I guess because I'll go back home then, back with my father." Jamie was uncertain of how to continue. "Louise said my dad had written about the flutes, but I thought he studied wolves. Are they connected? Is that how he met Louise?"

Ji-Min picked up a pebble and passed it from hand to hand a couple of times, then squared his shoulders and cleared his throat. "It's a long story."

"I'm sure it's more interesting than trying to milk the goats again," replied Jamie, hoping to ease the tension that had crept into the conversation.

Ji-Min smiled, tossing the pebble across the clearing, but his voice was serious when he spoke. "My mother died giving birth to Dai-Jeong. He had a nurse, but I was alone much of the time. I started roaming the woods around our home. It was in Ulchu, in southeastern Korea. There were mountains there, like these." Ji-Min nodded at the horizon. "I would run along the cliffs in the evenings. I started picking up things— rocks, fossils, once a spear point from an ancient midden pile. It made me feel better to find these things, not so alone."

Jamie shifted on the step. He knew exactly what his uncle meant—that was how he felt about his rocks.

"Anyway, one day I found a flute." Ji-Min patted his pouch. "The one I still carry. I learned to make music with it, but what really fascinated me were the carvings. I wanted to know why they were made, and who made them. I wanted to know what they meant." He stopped talking. After a moment, he stood and stretched.

The sun had dropped behind the cabin, and although it was still midafternoon the steps were in shadow. Jamie shivered, although it wasn't really that cold. He wrapped his arms around himself. Now that someone was ready to respond to his questions, he wasn't sure that he wanted to hear the answers.

"You look chilled. Would you like to go inside? We could

make some tea," Ji-Min said as he sat back down.

Jamie was tempted, but he remembered that his own flute was lying on the table and decided against it. "No. It's okay here."

Ji-Min was silent, seeming to sense Jamie's ambivalence.

Finally, Jamie took a deep breath and asked, "How old was my dad when you found the flute?"

"He was three or four, I think. I was almost sixteen. Our father had remarried by then. I went off to school in Seoul a short time later and never really went home again. I kept trying to figure out the meaning of the marks on the flute. One day, I found a photograph in an old archaeology book of some bone whistles with similar markings. Not exactly the same, but close enough. The flutes in the picture weren't Korean, though." He looked over at Jamie. "They were North American, from the Pacific Coast. From here. That's why I came."

Gus walked by and sat on Jamie's feet. Rather than push him away, the boy reached down and stroked the old rooster's scraggly feathers. Gus nibbled his fingers affectionately, then snuggled into the space between Jamie's ankles and closed his eyes.

Ji-Min smiled at the unlikely pair and kept talking. "Your father and I corresponded, and I told him about the marks on the flutes. He was a scholar even as a boy, and I urged him to come here to study. He secured a fellowship at the university when he was just seventeen. At first he researched archaic writing systems. I have some of his articles—I'll show them to you. He too hoped to figure out what the marks meant. The wolves came later."

"I've seen wolves here." Jamie adjusted his feet to accommodate the rooster's weight, and Gus squawked in protest.

Ji-Min stood up. "We should put him in the coop."

"Wait. How did you meet Louise? And my mother?"

"Louise was here. She grew up in these mountains."

"What about my mom?"

Ji-Min tossed another pebble across the clearing. When he spoke again, his voice was tight. "Your father met your mother at school. She was a linguist. They had classes together."

Jamie already knew this; somehow it didn't answer his question. "Why did they stop coming here?"

"Ask your father," Ji-Min replied. His tone was clipped, and he clenched his hands.

"Okay." Jamie was nervous. He couldn't figure out why his uncle was so upset. "Whatever you say." He tried to think of a comment that might soothe Ji-Min's sudden irritation. But before he could, he heard giggling. Cicely and Louise burst into the clearing, carrying packages and wearing new straw hats. Cicely's had a large silk rose pinned to it, and she had tucked a variety of wildflowers around the brim.

"How are Violet and Daisy? I sold all my goat cheese at the market," she said by way of greeting. "Did you have any trouble with the milking?"

Jamie moaned. He was suddenly aware of how much his ankle hurt.

"They're fine," Ji-Min answered. "They certainly are lively. And the milk, we drank every drop that was in the bucket."

Cicely grinned proudly and ran to her pets. Ji-Min and Louise exchanged a long look.

"I didn't say anything," said Ji-Min, and then he stomped after Cicely.

His aunt sat on the step next to Jamie and put her arms around him. "Louise," he said at last, "will you make me a cup of coffee?"

"Of course."

"I'm not going to drink it. I just want to hold the cup."

Nettle

CHAPTER 7

Son,

  Sa rang hae yo. I have enclosed the information you requested in your brief note.

  Louise writes that you injured your leg but that it is healing nicely. She also tells me you have met young Cicely (always a favorite of mine) and my brother. We have never spoken of him. Someday I will tell you why. I love him very much, but Jamie—trust Louise.

His aunt had given him the letter the night before, while Ji-Min and Cicely were at the pump doing dishes. Louise had seemed upset earlier in the evening when Ji-Min questioned Cicely's purchase of the hats. That, and something in the guarded way she passed Jamie the envelope, prompted him to slide it into his pocket without comment and open it later, only after he'd climbed up into the privacy of his loft.

Now, in the bright morning light, he read the note again. The marks along the bottom appeared to be identical to the ones in the letter he had lost. Jamie wished he could compare them to the designs on his flute, but the flute was downstairs. He wanted to do it when no one was watching. He slipped the letter inside the lacquered mandoo box.

Cicely sang as she prepared breakfast. The clatter of the manual eggbeater forced him out of bed. He couldn't eat bad pancakes two mornings in a row, especially since his aunt, for reasons unknown to him, had offered his goat-milking services to Cicely on a regular basis. He swung his legs out from under the pile of quilts and cringed. He'd forgotten about the pajamas.

"I have a present for you, Jamie," Cicely had said when she'd given them to him yesterday. "I bought hats for Louise and myself. But I know you don't have any pajamas—at least I never see you wash any." She blushed. "Anyway, these reminded me of you."

Now Jamie stared at his pale blue limbs. A trail of pink and yellow coffee cups led from his waist to his ankles. They fit better than the pair from Louise, but all in all, he liked the astronauts better. Downstairs the eggbeater started whirring again. "Hurry up," Jamie mumbled to himself. He jumped out of bed, still staring at his bizarrely clad legs, and smashed his head against the low, paneled ceiling. He heard a stifled giggle. By the time he finally clambered down the ladder, his stack of lumpy pancakes was on the table.

Cicely smiled. "Louise felt I should do more of the cooking since you'll be helping with the goats. I'm so glad you like Daisy and Violet."

He glanced at his aunt. Louise suddenly began cleaning burrs from the sleeve of her sweater.

"We can go milk them as soon as you're done with breakfast," Cicely continued.

"Might as well go now and get it over with," said Jamie sourly.

Cicely looked hurt.

"I don't want to eat anyway," he added.

Now she looked angry.

"I mean, I can hardly wait to see the goats—and I'm sure the pancakes will be just as good cold as they are hot."

Cicely left the cabin, and he followed her out to the pen. Louise flashed him a wicked grin as he passed, and Gus, waiting by the gate, cackled with anticipation.

When he had finished, there was a half bucket of milk, two large rips in his shirt, and a single long scratch down his cheek. Cicely said the ruined shirt didn't really count because

Jamie had done that himself, snagging it on some wire in his hurry to get away from the goats when they charged him.

He complained at dinner. "Look!" He pointed to his shirt.

Louise smiled serenely. "Excellent. Torn and dirty clothes are signs of a life well lived."

After two weeks the goats, though not friendly, tolerated him without protest. Cicely took a bit longer to master the pancakes, but eventually she managed to cook a batch that Jamie ate with pleasure, even accepting an offer of seconds. That morning, Louise slid him the maple syrup with a twinkle in her eye, and he had to acknowledge she had known what she was doing.

Ji-Min came occasionally, bringing game or fish. He was often accompanied by Ace, the large raven, who would caw with delight at the sight of Cicely.

The raven could hunt as well as it could catch pebbles. Jamie discovered this on the day that his uncle dragged a small deer into the clearing. "Ace found him," said Ji-Min, as Louise rushed to help skin and butcher the animal while Cicely hand-fed the bird chunks of the still-warm meat. Jamie turned away. His uncle, head bent to the work, complained about something. "He's not used to it. Let him go," Jamie heard his aunt reply as he climbed the low stair to the cabin.

In the weeks that followed, Louise worked long hours preparing for, as she put it, "the time of the heavy sky." Jamie was a little surprised by her seriousness. It was not quite mid-

August, and the days, though definitely growing shorter, still seemed long and languid. If he were home, he knew, he'd be at the community pool, the coming winter no more than a distant possibility.

Louise seemed to have a different sense of the seasons. In the mornings, after he and Cicely brought the wet laundry back from the stream, he watched his aunt pin it to the line. She stopped frequently and scanned the sky, as though looking for signs.

The drying racks that stood near the woodstove had been layered with delicate herbs. Larger bundles of branches hung from the rafters. Handmade willow baskets, filled with squash and onions from the garden, were packed into the root cellar behind the cabin, along with burdock and dandelion roots collected from the fields.

Once, Ji-Min questioned her about the surplus. "Why do you need to store all this food? You won't even be here this winter."

Jamie was surprised at this news, surprised as well by the anger in his uncle's voice. He glanced at his aunt.

She stiffened but replied calmly, "You never know—someone might be here."

Ji-Min stared at Louise for a long moment but said nothing.

Nor did Jamie. Although, he thought, that "someone" might well be her.

Louise continued to gather supplies. One day she woke

everyone early and packed a large picnic while Jamie and Cicely quickly took care of the animals. But what Jamie thought was going to be a day of playing and exploring was actually spent gathering sticky honeycombs.

"I spotted the swarm yesterday and followed them here," she said as Jamie hoisted himself up the limbs of a dead tree an hour's hike from the cabin. "It's late in the season. Honey's tastier if it's gathered in the spring, but I've almost run out."

Following her instructions, he reached his hand through an opening in the hollow trunk. "Won't I get stung?" He passed her a couple of pieces of honeycomb.

"No. You don't hear them, do you? They're not here."

"Louise?" Cicely looked at the sky. "Louise, I think the bees are coming back."

Jamie tossed down a few more chunks. He started to scramble down, but his hands, covered with honey, kept slipping. He was still a few feet from the ground when the swarm engulfed him. He jumped and ran, escaping with only a few stings. But his shirt, which had caught on a branch as he fell, was ruined. "I know, I know," he said without conviction. "It's the sign of a life well lived."

As they trudged home, Louise spotted a stand of blackberries and made them stop. They picked until dusk turned their blue-stained fingers gray. Jamie returned to the cabin stung, scratched, and grouchy. He grudgingly set out a dinner of leftovers while Cicely tended the animals. Louise stood over the woodstove and pressed the honey from the combs. She saved the beeswax. "I'll melt it down and mix in garlic, chamomile, and goldenseal. It's good to rub on cuts," she said. "Fights infection."

After they ate, Louise brought out the flutes. Jamie began to protest, but as she sat down and started to play, he saw the dark circles under her eyes and the uncharacteristic slump of her shoulders. Without another word he joined her, and Cicely picked up a pen.

When there was nothing else to do, he and Cicely made cheese.

"No, not like that," said Cicely one day as he poured the milk through a sieve. "You didn't get it hot enough."

"You're not this fussy about your pancakes."

"Pancakes!" She straightened up to make her point. "As far as I'm concerned, pancakes are just an excuse to eat syrup. But cheese . . ." She fixed him with a cold stare. "Cheese stands alone. You told me that."

"What? That was just a game." But he reheated the milk, unable to refute her weird logic. How could you argue with someone who accepted the words of "The Farmer in the Dell" as fact?

"No," Cicely said, as he tried it a second time. "Now you're going too fast. You have to pour slowly or you'll break up the curd."

Jamie sighed in exasperation. He knew she was right, but he was tired of working. He hadn't gone to the mountain since the accident. Louise had kept him too busy. And although he'd jogged a bit around the clearing, he'd not had time to try a longer run. He shifted restlessly from one foot to the other. I probably won't even be able to make the cross-country team, he thought. I'll be too out of shape.

"Steady—you're shaking." Cicely scraped the solids from the large sieve that Jamie was holding. "Stand still," she commanded.

Jamie slid his hands along the rim to get a better grip. He'd badly ripped another shirt the day before while helping Louise patch a hole in her roof. Now he was wearing the top from Cicely's coffee-cup pajamas. His hands against the light-blue flannel were a deep bronze after weeks in the sun, and his black hair, which he hadn't cut since spring, was pulled back with a leather strip in conscious imitation of his uncle. The thought of cross-country, in fact the thought of going back to school at all, made him queasy. It had been hard enough to fit in before; now—he glanced at his cuffs—it would be almost impossible.

"Jamie, pay attention!" Cicely shouted with such force that he dropped the sieve into the bowl of whey. The warm liquid splattered over his face and down the front of the pajama top and his jeans.

Louise came inside to see what the bickering was about. When she saw them glaring at each other, she started to laugh. "So, Jamie," she sputtered, "you take milk in your coffee after all. You should have told me!"

"He does look funny, doesn't he?" answered Cicely, her impatience with him giving way to amusement.

Jamie stared at them, trying to think of a suitably hostile rebuttal. "I'm funny?" he began as he wiped milk from his chin. "You two . . ." He rubbed his hands on the front of the pajamas, then bent down and used a sleeve to dry his feet.

"Yes?"

He looked up at them. They were smiling at him with such obvious affection that he was taken aback. He swallowed his angry words. It would be hard to go back to Seattle all right, and not just because of what he'd find on his return. He realized that what was really upsetting him was the thought of leaving this place behind.

Louise helped them clean up. "I think this batch is spoiled," she said, swirling what was left in the bowl.

Jamie was uncomfortable. He knew he should feel some remorse, but in honesty, he was relieved to be done with cheese making for the day.

Louise seemed to sense his mood. "You know, I think I can finish things up here by myself. But I would really like some mulberries, and the only bushes I know of are out near the end of the mountain trail. Would you mind very much if I asked you to go and get some for me?"

"No. Not at all!" Jamie ran to the door, then glanced

expectantly at Cicely. She turned to Louise.

Louise nodded. "You'd better go with him. I don't think he realizes it yet, but he has no idea what a mulberry bush looks like."

Cicely hugged Louise and ran out into the clearing after Jamie. They walked the trail side by side, Jamie stepping behind Cicely whenever the path narrowed. He noticed how quietly she moved, and tried to place his feet as lightly as she did without much success. They took their time getting to the mountain. Cicely pointed out many "landmarks" Jamie had missed when he'd run the trail alone: small hollows of rainwater, fallen branches shaped like snakes, a large moss-covered rock that looked just like Louise's green-velvet reading chair. Seen through Cicely's eyes, the woods seemed magical, and the dark shadowy places that had once frightened Jamie now shimmered with possibility.

"Look at those big mushrooms. I think they're poisonous. Don't they look like my first few batches of pancakes?"

"Yes. Yes they do, although the mushrooms might taste better." Jamie was laughing as they stepped from the trees into bright sunshine. The mountain rose up a short distance in front of them. The strip of silk fabric was still tied to the tree, although the bright red was faded now to nearly pink. Jamie, suddenly serious, said, "This is where I hurt my leg." He shifted his weight uncomfortably.

Cicely nodded and pointed up the face of the mountain.

"Yes, it was that boulder."

Jamie was surprised she knew. He wondered what his aunt had told her. Ace swooped down from somewhere, and Cicely ran off after the bird before Jamie could ask her.

"I've got the berries," she said when she returned. She put down the basket Louise had given them. "This is where you like to dig, isn't it? Where do you get the tools?" she asked. "How do you clean the dirt off the rocks?"

At first he thought she was just being polite. "Are you really interested in this?" he asked at one point.

"Yes." She paused for a moment, and he watched her struggle to find the words for what she was thinking. "I know about studying things: the weather, the trees, other animals. They help me figure out what is happening, or what just happened. But I never thought about studying things to see what happened a long time ago. Up until this summer, until I started talking to you, I never really thought about the past. Or the future."

He had been ready to make fun of her comment about "other animals," but she had such a sad look on her face that he didn't have the heart to tease her. Instead, he showed her the way he dug around promising-looking "bumps," using his fingertips and stopping frequently to blow away the loose soil.

Cicely practiced this technique, but she kept using her fingers like claws, raking the earth with her nails.

"No, like this," Jamie said gently, reaching over and

straightening her fingers slightly.

She tried again.

He watched, prepared to reach for her hand once more, and was disappointed when she did it correctly.

Cicely bent her head close to the ground and blew. She had tucked her long hair behind her ears, but now it slid forward over her shoulder and hid her face, like a curtain darkening the stage at the end of a play. Jamie felt his throat tighten. He tried to say something but could manage only a strangled-sounding cough.

"Wasn't that okay?" Cicely pushed her hair back and studied him for a moment. She stood suddenly and brushed the dirt from her hands. "C'mon," she said as she grabbed the basket of berries. "Let's run. I'll race you."

She was off before he could reply. At the start of the trail, she waited for him, hopping from one foot to the other. They started back to the cabin together. Jamie held back at first, not wanting to pull too far ahead. Cicely, though, seemed to match his stride easily. He glanced over at her. She didn't even seem winded, despite the fact that she was carrying the basket. Ignoring the twinge in his ankle, he pushed himself to go faster.

He managed to enter the clearing a step or two in front of her, but he couldn't really consider it much of a victory. He was gasping for breath. She was laughing.

"Arggh." Jamie rubbed his leg, "I should have been training. I probably won't even make the team."

"Don't worry, you're much faster than you were when we ran together last spring."

"What?"

"No, it's true. I had so much fun then. I've been telling Louise that I'd love to go back there with you." Suddenly Cicely stopped laughing. Jamie followed her gaze and saw his aunt and uncle standing on the step of the cabin, a large bucket of freshly caught trout wedged between them.

"What did you say?" barked Ji-Min. "Come inside."

Cicely started to cry. Jamie reached out and took her arm. She shook free and ran toward the cabin. He started to follow her through the door but was stopped by Louise, who told him to round up the chickens.

Dinner was quiet. Jamie spoke a couple of times. Cicely would look up at the sound of his voice, then quickly drop her eyes in response to a cold stare from Ji-Min. Louise didn't speak, but despite Ji-Min's forbidding countenance, she met his gaze throughout the meal; and once, passing the potatoes, she patted Jamie's hand reassuringly.

Jamie volunteered to do the dishes. No one objected. He leaned against the pump and plunged his hands into the pail of cold water. The plates clattered against the edge of the bucket. He could still hear the voices from inside.

"She wants to go back with him? What does she mean?"

"She's young, Ji-Min. She should have the same

opportunities we did, the same chance to decide—"

"No!" Ji-Min interrupted. "What if he . . . "

Jamie couldn't hear the rest of Ji-Min's comment.

"Jamie has worked hard. He's ready to help you. But I don't feel comfortable having him play the flute if he doesn't know what it will do," said Louise.

"That woman kept him from here too long." Something banged against the table. "He'll never believe it, never figure it out in time. Our way is so different from what he knows. Tonight—it has to be tonight."

"But—"

"I don't care. I won't let her go with him."

Jamie didn't like this side of his uncle. He reached up and untied the leather strip from his hair and tossed it to the ground. Through the window, he saw Ji-Min rest his head against the table. Louise reached out to him and put her hand on his shoulder, an unreadable expression on her face. She looked outside, and her eyes met Jamie's briefly before she looked away. He rinsed the last dish. After a quick look to make sure he wasn't being watched, Jamie bent down, grabbed the long strip of leather, and stuffed it into his pocket. He went back inside.

Cicely was already lying on her mat. Jamie couldn't tell from the rise and fall of the thick quilts whether she was asleep or crying again.

"Here," said Ji-min, tossing a stack of magazines on the

table. "These are for you. They're some of your father's articles. I told you I would bring them. I keep my word." He fingered the pouch at his waist. "What about you? Will you play for me? You said you would. What about the piece of music you played the night we met?"

Jamie was ready to say yes. He thought it might get Cicely out of trouble if he cooperated. He moved toward the table, where his flute lay near the pile of papers. Just as he was about to reach for the wolf whistle, he saw his aunt standing behind Ji-Min. "No," she mouthed, shaking her head slightly. *Trust Louise.* Dai-Jeong had written that to Jamie twice. He glanced from his aunt to his uncle. *Trust Louise.* Jamie reached past the flute and picked up the magazines. He climbed the ladder to bed.

It was too dark to read, but Jamie couldn't sleep. Sometime later he heard arguing, then two sets of footsteps cross the room and leave the cabin. Louise must have gone with Ji-Min. He thought about going down to Cicely, to ask her about what she had said. But he didn't. He realized he already knew what she'd meant. "Last spring." He remembered her words. Last spring he had run with the wolves.

Radish

CHAPTER 8

. . . *occurrences of these flutes, or "wolf whistles," in the coastal mountain regions of present-day Korea and western Canada provide archaeological evidence of migrations of hunter societies along the Bering Shelf, between the Asian land mass and the Pacific Coast of North America.*

These flutes, usually made from the femur of a crane or eagle, are invariably carved with hundreds of ornate designs. The flutes are often found buried along with the bones of both wolves and humans. The significance

of this juxtaposition of artifacts in a single
burial site remains unclear, as does the exact
meaning of the carved symbols. Further stud-
ies are needed if . . .

—Park Dai-Jeong
Journal of Archaeological
Analysis

Jamie reread the paragraph. He wished he had a dictionary. He'd awakened early and paged through the papers Ji-Min had left the night before, quickly marking the articles written by his father. Now, in hopes of figuring out what was going on, he was reading through them carefully. Or trying to.

He put the journal down and stared out the window. No noise from downstairs. He sniffed: no coffee. Louise must not have come back yet. But he should have heard Cicely—she was always up early. Jamie slipped out from under the quilts and climbed down the ladder.

There was no sign of Cicely's mat, and her quilts were folded in a neat pile at the end of Louise's bed. Her straw hat was still hanging near the door, but the small covered basket she had brought with her the first night was gone.

"Cicely? Louise?" Jamie ran outside. "Louise!"

Somewhere behind the cabin an ax cracked against a piece of wood. Jamie followed the sound. His aunt stood in front of one of the small outbuildings that were scattered around the clearing. The bushel of trout was balanced on a low step, and a large stack of wood was piled at her feet. She looked up as he rounded the corner.

"Help me split this wood. We need to smoke the trout before it spoils."

"Where's Cicely?"

"Jamie, I need to get this ready." Her eyes were red and sagged at the corners.

"Have you been crying? Where's Cicely?"

"No, it's from the smoke. Here, give me a hand."

There wasn't any smoke. The fire wasn't going yet. "Louise—"

"I know, Jamie," she interrupted. "We have to get this going first."

"What about the animals? Shouldn't I check them?"

"I fed the chickens already." She leaned on the ax handle and looked away from Jamie before she continued. "And the goats are gone. Ji-Min took them when he and Cicely left."

"She didn't leave—she wanted to come with me. He took her." Jamie felt the anger rise in his stomach. His mouth filled with the taste of metal.

"Yes, he took her."

"Why didn't you stop him?"

Jamie watched his aunt struggle to respond. At last, her voice husky, she said, "I would have if I were sure he was wrong. Perhaps I should have. It has not been our custom—

mine or Cicely's—to question Ji-Min. But I think this time I should have." She stared into the trees.

"But Louise." Jamie was nearly shrieking. "My father told me to trust you! How could you have let this happen?"

"Jamie, please. We all want to believe in an absolute right and wrong. It's easier that way. But it isn't always that clear. What's right for an individual may not be what's best for the group." She split another log. "Without the goats, I won't be able to make cheese. And I won't be getting any more game from Ji-Min."

Jamie noted the finality in her voice and wondered if she *had* tried to stop his uncle.

She swung the ax behind her shoulder and brought it down through a large chunk of hickory. "It's going to be a hard winter. I need this trout."

He stepped forward and picked up a second ax. Matching his aunt swing for swing, Jamie pictured his uncle each time he split a log.

"All right. That's okay, but try to get them flat. And flip them so they are facing head to tail." Louise was showing Jamie how to spread the trout on the slatted shelves that lined three walls of the smokehouse, floor to ceiling. "You'll have to stretch to reach the top ones."

"Like this?"

"Yes, good. Just a little more space between them so

the smoke can circulate."

He shifted the fish a bit.

"Perfect. I'll hand them in to you, okay? It will go faster."

They soon fell into a comfortable rhythm. Jamie stretched his left hand out the doorway, where Louise stood ready to pass a trout to him. Without even turning to look at her, he grabbed it, switched the fish to his right hand, and placed it on a shelf.

He shoved the fish slightly so it would slide back, then reached his index finger up between the slats to coax the fish into place. His mind started to wander, going back over the events that had led to Cicely's departure. "Louise, yesterday when I was with Cicely . . ."

"Careful, Jamie."

The last four fish were tail first and overlapping. Without a word, he placed them correctly and brought his thoughts back to the smokehouse.

They were nearing the end of the job. Jamie bent close to the ground to reach the bottom shelf. He was bracing himself against the side of the shed for balance when he heard something. At first, he thought it was the fabric of his jeans rubbing against the wall. Then he heard it again, a sort of muffled growl from somewhere near the shed. He glanced up but couldn't see past Louise standing in the doorway.

"Keep working." Her voice was low and soft.

Jamie reached out for another fish. The growl drew closer.

"Keep working." Another fish.

Jamie was nervous. "Is it a wolf?"

Louise didn't even look over her shoulder. "It's your uncle. And I'd rather not talk to him right now."

A twig snapped, some leaves rustled nearby. But the next time he heard the growl, it had moved away from the shed.

Louise wiped her hands on the front of her sweater. "That's it. Now for the fire." She showed him how to sort the wood they'd cut: twigs and branches for tinder; split logs for steady burning; a small amount of green wood for slowing the flames.

There was a shallow bowl-shaped indentation in the dirt floor of the smokehouse. Jamie watched as she built a neat pyramid, twig by twig.

"There, that's perfect." She stood and brushed her hands clean. "Now you try." She kicked the pile to pieces.

Jamie gasped.

"It's one thing to watch me do it, something else altogether to do it yourself."

Jamie had been sitting on the step. He stood and switched places with Louise. She leaned against the doorframe watching. "Better." She nodded after his third attempt. "Just tuck a little loose bark on the far side and we're ready."

"I suppose you're going to make me light it by knocking stones together?"

"Hmm, I hadn't thought of that."

Jamie had been joking, and was taken aback to see that she

was considering the option.

"No, I guess not. Not today. I've got to get this started and banked before evening." She pulled a box of matches from her pocket. "I'll need to watch the fire for a bit, but why don't you go inside and get some food and a bottle of the cider we pressed? We can eat out here. And talk."

Jamie stared nervously around the corner.

"No, it's okay. He's gone, Jamie."

He cautiously stepped into the clearing. No wolves, no uncle. Just the empty goat pen. He stood and stared at it for a moment, using his hand to shield his eyes from the sun. "Yuck." He gasped at the fish smell on his fingers. He headed for the pump before going inside and, figuring Louise was as much in need of a wash as he was, filled a pail with water and carried it back to her.

She didn't hear him coming, and he was surprised to see her hunched on the step with her head buried in her arms. The bucket sloshed as Jamie gently lowered it to the ground, but Louise didn't look up. He tiptoed back to the cabin.

He thought briefly of trying to make coffee, but the wood-stove had not been lit. Instead he decided to bring what was left in the pot from yesterday. He put it in a basket along with some cider, two mugs, a nearly ripe tomato from the win-dowsill, and a half loaf of wheat bread sweetened with honey.

He looked at the tray of small cheeses. Cicely had planned to make a trip to the market with these. She'd told Jamie that she hoped to buy Louise a colorful scarf, and some bells for Daisy and Violet. She had winked at him as she discussed her plans, and he had known she had something in mind for him as well. At the time he'd groaned at the prospect of another garish gift from Cicely, but now he mourned the loss of the unknown object, no matter how useless it might have been. He picked up the cheese closest to him. With it in one hand and the basket in the other, he left the cabin. He hooked the door with his foot and pulled it shut behind him.

Louise had started the fire in his absence. "Come quick, Jamie. Breathe the first smoke—it's the spirit of the fire." She threw a handful of sage and rosemary onto the flames.

"Dad says something like that when he cooks." Jamie stuck his head into the smokehouse and took a deep breath.

Louise rinsed her hands in the bucket, then splashed water on her face. "Thank you for thinking of this. It was very sweet of you."

He shrugged but was pleased she'd noticed.

Louise rummaged through the basket. "Oh, you are clever today," she said, pulling out the coffee. She shoved the tin pot next to the burning logs, waited a few minutes, then poured herself a mug before sitting down next to Jamie.

"Dad says the steam is the spirit of the food."

"He is a wise man."

They sat quietly for a moment.

"Jamie, do you want to go home? Dai-Jeong is expecting

me to drive you back to Seattle in a week or so, in time for the start of school. I'd take you now—but I'm worried about Cicely. I'd like to wait a bit, in case she manages . . ." She cleared her throat. "I could call your dad, though. He would come for you if you wanted."

"No." Jamie hoped he sounded convincing. In truth, he suddenly longed for his father. "No, I want to help as much as I can."

She smiled gratefully but said, "Let me know if you change your mind. I could call him tomorrow. I have to go into town anyway and sell the last of the cheeses." She took the one Jamie was still holding and spread a little on a chunk of bread. This she handed to him before she made another piece for herself. "And I have to sell the chickens."

Jamie stopped chewing. "Not Gus. You can't get rid of Gus."

"It's going to be a cold winter, and I . . . Jamie, I don't know what's ahead for me—or Cicely. I may have to leave. There may not be time to take care of the chickens."

"But Gus is not a chicken."

"Well, I know that, Jamie. He's a roo—"

"No, I mean he's not just a chicken, and not just a rooster either. He's my friend. You can't get rid of him." Jamie's voice grew louder as he spoke. Gus, hearing the commotion, came around the back side of the cabin to see what was wrong. He stood near Jamie and pecked at his shoelace. Jamie picked him up and glared at Louise.

"But Jamie . . . "

"No. You can't get rid of him. Just because he's an animal, you feel he can't be my friend. You're wrong, Louise. You're really wrong! The animals aren't so different from us. They're not."

Louise had been ready to argue with Jamie but looked startled after his last comment. "You're right," she said after a moment. "You're right about the animals. And if anyone should know it, I should."

Jamie squeezed Gus so hard, the rooster squawked, but Jamie didn't let go.

"But we need to do something with him. He can't stay here through the winter and survive."

"I'm taking him back to Seattle with me." Gus squawked again.

"Jamie, you can't take a noisy, opinionated old rooster to live in Seattle."

"Of course not," said Jamie calmly. "I wouldn't dream of doing that. But I am going to take Gus."

They stared at each other for a moment.

"All right." Louise rolled her eyes. "I have too much on my mind to argue about this. Let your dad figure it out." She stood up and carefully placed a few more branches on the fire, then stepped back and watched the smoke circle before it faded into the sky.

Jamie squeezed Gus again. The rooster, though fond of him, had endured enough of this form of affection. With a loud shriek he began flapping his wings, then bit Jamie on the nose. Jamie, startled, dropped the flailing bird. Gus clawed the boy's chest to keep from falling, and succeeded in shredding the front of Jamie's shirt.

Louise laughed till tears ran down her face. "I'm sorry, Jamie."

"It's my last T-shirt."

"You're absolutely right. Bring Gus to Seattle. It's just what Dai-Jeong needs to add a little excitement to his scholarly life." She sat down and poured another cup of coffee. "Who knows? He might even switch from wolves to roosters."

Jamie rubbed his nose, then sat down next to her and grabbed another chunk of bread. "Why did Dad pick wolves anyway? It doesn't seem connected to linguistics."

Louise shrugged. "Well, I guess one thing led to another. Your mother stayed with linguistics, and your father moved on. I know they felt their work was related."

Jamie nodded. "I looked at the articles Ji-Min left. There was one about the flutes."

Louise stood and put a few green logs on the fire, along with some sage and juniper branches. "See, I want to keep the fire going like this, not blazing, but a slow, steady heat."

"How come you didn't want me to play the flute for Ji-Min last night? I think he took Cicely because I wouldn't play for him." Jamie took a stick and started to trace lines in the dirt; he couldn't figure out how to tell Louise what else he thought about Ji-Min and Cicely.

"No, you mustn't think it was your fault. Cicely was going to leave soon anyway. As for the flute, well . . ."

He looked up to find Louise staring at him.

"Jamie, how much music have you studied in school?"

He shrugged. "You mean history and stuff? Not much. We have lots of music at home, though."

"In earlier times, ancient times, music was more than entertainment; it was used for the expression of ideas and beliefs. No form of communication was more important. Do you understand? With words, people could talk only to each other. But through music, they felt they could communicate with animals as well; that they could, in fact, become like those animals, given enough practice and concentration."

Jamie thought Louise was trying to dodge his question. "I'm talking about last night, not ancient history. Why didn't you want me to play the flute?"

"I know you're upset. I'm trying to tell you. Just because your school hasn't taught you these things doesn't mean they're not true."

"What? Are you telling me that music can turn someone into an animal? I doubt it," he snorted. But her words made him uncomfortable.

"Jamie." Louise appeared frustrated. "Do you know they

use sound waves in medicine all the time to change matter?
A doctor trains for a long time, manipulates a tool that gen-
erates a certain frequency, modulates it depending on the
requirements of the patient, and—*zap!*—she breaks a kidney
stone apart. Why is it so hard to imagine that with the right
kind of training, that same doctor couldn't use sound fre-
quencies to pull the stone back together? Do you think any of
your teachers could start a fire with two rocks?" She blew on
the kindling and it flared briefly; her eyes reflected the dart-
ing sparks. "Still thinking? It doesn't matter. Whether your
teachers could do it or not, stones can start a fire. And
whether you believe it or not, music is powerful. Even if only
a few of us remember the old ways, what was true remains
true."

"But we don't need music to communicate now—we have
writing," Jamie answered stubbornly.

"The people who first made the flutes had writing too.
You're right. It is a powerful tool, and the flute makers knew
it." She took a stick and and traced the marks he'd drawn in
the sand. She added a line here and there until they resembled
the marks at the bottoms of his father's letters. "They used
writing to decorate the flutes. Did you know your mother had
been trying to decipher these marks? Your uncle thought she
had figured it out."

"Ji-Min didn't like my mother."

"He did. Once."

"He sounded so mean when he talked about her last night. And he took Cicely away. I wanted to be like him, but . . ." Jamie jabbed his stick into the center of the fire.

"You are like him, Jamie, more than you know." Louise watched the flame flicker brightly, then die down. "Ji-Min is responsible for a number of . . ." She seemed to be choosing her words with unusual consideration. "That is, Cicely is not the only one he takes care of. He did what he thought was best."

"I don't want to talk about it anymore. I wouldn't have played for him last night anyway."

Gus had been squawking all this time. Now he started poking at the food basket. Jamie broke off a corner of bread and fed it to the rooster.

"Forgiven him already?" asked his aunt.

"Well, he didn't really do anything wrong. He was just being himself."

"Yes," she said quietly. "Exactly. Someday you'll understand."

Phlox

CHAPTER 9

Folk narratives from many cultures attribute to wolves a unique balance of individual power and group identity. This duality, far from being a whimsical or fictional construct, is borne out by the most rigorous field studies: Within wolf society, the strongest hunter feeds the weak, all adults teach the cubs, and the pack leader serves the needs of the group even when it demands brutality or physical injury to a group member.

—Park Dai-Jeong
International Zoological Review

Jamie looked up from the magazine and checked the fire. He tucked a bit of green wood near the edge closest to him and threw a handful of sage into the flames, watching the smoke curl from the hole in the roof of the shed and swirl up into the golden light of late afternoon. He picked up the magazine again and flipped through the pages, trying to find his place. The description reminded him of Ji-Min: a good hunter who shares his food and raises someone else's child. And what was it Louise had said about him taking Cicely? That he had acted that way because he had others to take care of.

He shifted uncomfortably at the thought of his uncle. Jamie had seen the brutal side too. He hoped Louise would be home soon. He'd expected her back by now, but, he reminded himself, she'd gotten a late start. It had taken a long time to get the chickens into crates. Even after wedging all the boxes into the back of the car, Louise had seemed reluctant to go. Although it was a warm morning, she made sure that Jamie knew how to start a fire in the cabin's wood-stove, and that he knew how to damp the flames in the smokehouse for the night.

"Tomorrow we'll pack the fish away for storage, but I might as well show you how to do it now," she said, after explaining (for the sixth time) how to tuck the green wood into the fire to slow the flames.

"Louise, you should go." He could hear the chickens protesting. "I can learn how to do it later." Actually, Jamie was not interested in handling the fish again. He hoped to escape this job, but Louise was insistent. She carefully demonstrated how to place the trout in a long wooden box, separating each row with a thick layer of coarse salt.

"Fill the buckets with water, all of them, and bring them inside," she called as she was leaving. "You never know when you'll be thirsty."

"But Louise," Jamie said in surprise. She was usually frugal in her use of water.

"Do it."

He grabbed four large metal buckets and walked to the pump. He'd heard her leave the cabin during the night, and heard her crying after she'd returned. He didn't want to risk upsetting her again. As he filled the last bucket, he heard the Volvo turn over and the sound of the complaining chickens gradually fade into the distance.

Now, Jamie looked up from the magazine and checked the angle of the sun. "Still some time before dark," he said to comfort himself. He was about to resume reading when he heard a noise in the thicket of brush that flanked the back of the smokehouse. He tensed and craned his neck in that direction.

"Oh, Ace. I'm glad it's you." Jamie relaxed as the raven hopped into the clearing. "What's new?"

The bird tilted his head and looked at Jamie with one eye and then the other.

"Do you want to play catch?" Jamie threw a pebble into the air, but Ace ignored it. He hopped closer to Jamie.

"Sorry, I don't have any treats. I know Cicely always feeds you, but Cicely's gone. Ji-Min took her away, but he shouldn't have. She didn't do anything. Louise is gone too, but she should be back soon." Jamie threw another pebble.

The raven stared at him, then rose up into the air. He dipped a wing before soaring over the trees.

Jamie continued to read, straining a bit to make out the print in the fading light:

> *Wolves, though sometimes brutal, have a great capacity for what we would call "play." Packs have been observed engaging in a variety of running and wrestling games. Even more remarkable is the range of cooperative activities, including tag, catch, and hide-and-go-seek, engaged in by wolves and ravens. In addition to playing together, these two species often form hunting alliances: the raven scouting out prey, then alerting the pack to its location by means of a call or a tipped wing, in exchange for a share of the carrion and protection from other scavengers.*

Ace circled back over the clearing and landed a few feet from the smokehouse. Jamie watched the bird. Tag; catch; hide-and-go-seek—those were the games that Cicely played with her raven. He thought of how the bird would call to her, then tip a wing as though beckoning the girl to follow. And he remembered how Cicely would always set aside part of her dinner for Ace, no matter how hungry she was. Jamie shuddered. Even with all the evidence, it was still hard to think of Cicely as a wolf. Jamie shook his head. It didn't matter— Cicely was gone. Or was she? Jamie realized he'd never seen Ace unless Cicely was around.

"Ace?" he whispered. "Where is she?" The bird pecked at the ground. "No, Ace, really. Where is she? It's important." The bird cocked his head and stared at him. Jamie tried not to squirm as the raven scrutinized him. Finally Ace relaxed. He seemed to have decided something. Cawing softly, he hopped toward the thicket. Jamie stood and quietly walked after the bird. He peered into the dense brush; a twig snapped and there was a sudden flash of gold. Jamie plunged into the underbrush and reached toward the movement. He grabbed a fistful of fur and dug his fingers into warm flesh. "Cicely? . . . Cicely, is that you?"

Something whined, then yelped. Jamie jumped and let go as a shadow passed over him. Whatever had been hiding in the brambles scurried away as he leaped to his feet and stumbled into Louise.

"It's me," she said. "Don't be frightened."

Jamie struggled to get his breath.

His aunt eyed him with some concern. "Were you nervous alone here today? I have some packages in the car—come and help me get them."

"No."

Louise shot him a surprised look.

"I mean, yes, I'll help you, but . . . I was just reading this article my dad wrote about wolves, and I, well . . ."

"Tell me, Jamie. Tell me what you're thinking."

Ace cawed somewhere overhead.

"Louise." He swallowed. "Last fall, when my mother was sick, I thought I heard wolves chasing me when I ran. I heard them after she died, too, when I ran in the spring. And then, the other day, Cicely told me that *she* ran with me last spring. I think the reason Ji-Min got so mad is that he heard her say it." He sucked a scratch on his hand.

"Go on."

"Sometimes I even thought I felt the wolves, nipping at me, you know." Jamie looked directly at his aunt. He knew by now she would not lie. "Do you think I imagined it?"

She didn't look away. After what seemed like a long time, she cleared her throat and, speaking slowly, replied, "No, I wouldn't say that at all."

Jamie sighed. "My mom believed me, too."

"You told her?" His aunt's voice was tight.

He nodded. "She said they were my family. I thought she was confused because she was so ill, and well, you know . . . I didn't understand what she meant then, but now I think I do. It's true, isn't it?"

Louise looked shocked. "All these weeks we wondered what you would think, wondered how to tell you about us without frightening you away. And you already knew. Why didn't Dai-Jeong tell me?"

Jamie was surprised to hear the anger in her voice. "He didn't know." He quickly defended his father. "My mom told me not to say anything to him."

Jamie watched her face color.

She grabbed him by the shoulders. "Jamie, my God, what was she thinking? Why didn't she tell you everything?"

"What do you mean? Let go of me."

"What do you think I mean?" Her voice had gotten louder. "Did you listen to what I said yesterday about music? What do you think the flutes are for? Why do you think you are here?"

Jamie, frightened by the intensity of her voice, tried to pull away, but she held on.

"We've waited all summer for you to figure this out. Can't you see? Is it too late for you to understand this? Ji-Min is right—we never should have let you stay away so long." Her lip curled over her clenched teeth.

"Leave me alone," he cried.

Louise let go. She was panting. She started to speak but then turned suddenly and ran off through the woods.

Jamie stood and watched her pass between two large pines. He stared at those trees for a long time without moving, without thinking, waiting for her to come back. When it got too dark to see the trees, he damped the fire exactly the way she had told him to, put Gus in the coop, and filled each chicken's water and food container even though there were no more chickens. He walked down the path to where the old Volvo was parked and grabbed as many of the packages as he could carry. Then, tripping occasionally as he walked along the deeply shadowed trail, he returned to the clearing and went inside the cabin.

Wild Blackberry

CHAPTER 10

My dear Louise,

I miss Jamie. The days have passed so slowly in his absence. I am sorry he did not write to me more often; I would have liked to share in his observations of life with you. He has the makings of a good scientist: an excellent eye for details, and the imagination to shape those details into something with life and form. (I imagine you are smiling as you read this. Yes, despite the fact he has pulled away from me, I remain the proud father.)

You are sure you do not want me to come

for him? I would love to see young Cicely.
I always felt close to her. I am glad she and
Jamie are friends. And although it is painful
given Jamie's coolness to me, I am also glad
to hear that he has taken to my brother. Ji-
Min is a good teacher. I should know. But
do watch them. I couldn't bear it if anything
happened. Have you spoken with Jamie
about how things stand? Are you sure you
don't want me to come? Perhaps, if I were
there, we could all talk and . . .

No, I am sure you are right, it is best if
I stay away. Please forgive me for wishing
it were otherwise. Remind Jamie that I will
come for him if he calls.

Dai-Jeong

The letter smelled faintly of garlic and ginger.

"Dad." Jamie was crying as the first soft lines of morning light shimmered on the floor. *"Ah-ba."* He looked out the window and rubbed his eyes. He slipped the note back into the pile of things he'd taken from the Volvo. He could imagine what Louise would say if she returned to the cabin and found him reading her mail.

Jamie got up from the table and walked around the room, opening drawers and cupboards in search of food: one apple, a stale biscuit, a half pot of yesterday's coffee. He turned back to the packages from the car and hesitated only briefly before opening them. Better to deal with the possibility of Louise's wrath later than to starve now. Matches, three pairs of woolen socks, a large bag of coarse salt, coffee beans. Not much of a breakfast. There had to be something else. Louise always came back with a few treats. (He smiled as he recalled the elaborate chocolate cake that had once, unexpectedly, followed a meal of dandelion greens and mushrooms.) Maybe he had missed something in the car; after all, it had been dark.

Jamie grabbed one of Louise's old sweaters from a hook near the door and went outside. He looked around the clearing apprehensively. It didn't make him feel any better that Louise had not returned. She was either injured or still angry with him.

"Louiiiise!" Jamie's voice echoed through the trees. He edged his way to the outhouse, looking over his shoulder after nearly every step.

He relaxed a bit as he washed at the pump. The water was so cold that it was hard to think, let alone worry. As he headed for the path to the Volvo, he paused briefly in front of the chicken coop. Gus was moving around inside. "I'll get you on my way back," Jamie shouted as he passed. "Eat some of the food I put out for your ex-roomates last night." Jamie started to run. He glanced up as he approached a hill along the path. From the top of this rise there was an open view of distant mountains that Jamie loved. Today, as he looked at the sky, he stumbled over something lying on the ground.

He bent down and picked up a mottled gray stone the size and shape of a sparrow. His mom would have liked it. She always liked the rocks that looked like something else. He slipped it in a sweater pocket and grinned.

Jamie adjusted his stride slightly to accommodate the weight of the rock. He settled back into an easy rhythm and recalled a conversation he'd had with his mother last fall. She had been at one end of their lumpy couch, resting. He was leaning against the other end, studying French, and he had, without realizing it, begun to speak out loud.

"*J'espère. Tu espères.*"

"Yes, I do." His mother smiled.

Jamie had been momentarily perplexed by her response. "Hope," he said. "It means *hope* in French. You know: I hope, you hope . . ."

"Yes, that's what I meant. I do hope."

"I didn't know you spoke French. You could have been helping me with my homework."

"Oh, I don't. There is an old English word, *espeire*, that also means hope. It's a bit obsolete now, but still worth learning. She smiled. "Both words have the same Latin root: *sperare*."

Jamie rolled his eyes in mock horror.

His mother kept talking. "It's almost the same as the Latin word *spirare*, to breathe, and that's the root of *spirit*, *respirate*, *inspire*, and *aspire*. You won't find it in the dictionary, but I think that if we could look back far enough, we'd find that all these words are related—that hope is tied to life and breath and action."

"What else?" he asked.

"Well, in my opinion . . ." They both laughed. "Spiral— there is hope in every small green shoot that spirals toward the sun."

"And *despair* too, right? It must have the same root. And that's what I'm going to do if I don't get this homework done."

"Yes, *despair*, too. But don't, Jamie. Don't despair. Guard the small green shoot, keep it alive." She closed her eyes then and leaned back against the pillows. Jamie reached out and grabbed her hand. "I still hope," she whispered.

Jamie smiled now as he remembered how much she loved fooling around with words. It was the first time since his mother's death that he had been able to think of her without crying. "'Guard the small green shoot.' What a crazy thing to say." He shook his head, but he knew exactly what she had meant. "I will, Mom." He looked at the sky as he ran. "I will."

Jamie rounded the last bend in the path, then stopped short at the sight of the Volvo. The front door hung open. Bags and boxes were scattered on the ground. Jamie crept cautiously toward the car. He remembered closing that door last night; his arms had been full and he had twisted awkwardly to slam it shut with his hip. Louise could have come back to the car. It was like her to leave the car open; she was always leaving cupboards ajar and drawers pulled out. But she would never litter. Never.

Maybe the door hadn't quite latched when he'd bumped it and the wind had blown it open, or maybe an animal had wedged through the crack and gotten in. Jamie edged closer. Piles of papers and packages spilled over the seats. He reached in and grabbed a large bag of what looked like chocolate chips, uncovering some dried fruit and a box of beeswax candles. Jamie hoisted the bag of chocolate against his hip, cradling it there with one hand, and stuffed the smaller items into the empty pocket of Louise's sweater.

He was about to search the backseat when he heard something crashing through the woods. He ducked, then dropped to his knees as the sound—and whatever was making it—came closer. Peering under the Volvo, beyond its rusty muffler and the tailpipe lashed up with a length of rope, he saw a pair of legs. Louise? Did she have pants that color? Maybe. He'd never really paid attention to what she looked like from the knees down.

Jamie braced himself against the side of the car, adjusting his position to get a better look. It was Louise. He was about to call out when a second person ran into the clearing. "Cicely!" His cry ripped the morning air. Still clutching the bag of chocolate, he struggled to stand, slipped, and cracked his head against the corner of the open car door.

His cry was muffled by the sudden sound of a flute from somewhere behind him. The dissonant melody was played with a richness and precision that, for a moment, made him forget what was happening around him. His mind followed the pattern of notes, and he forgot his confusion and fear and hunger as he listened. He even forgot the pain in his head. The fingers of his free hand moved up and down involuntarily, covering the holes of an imaginary flute.

Jamie turned to the sound. He saw Ji-Min, the flute in his hands, standing a few feet away. He tried to decipher the look on his uncle's face: calm, with no trace of the anger from the other night. But Jamie saw no warmth there either; the man's expression was blank. He had masked any trace of what he was thinking.

As the music ended, Cicely screamed, "You promised. You promised you wouldn't do this to her until she said it was okay." Her voice was wild.

Jamie, still wedged between the car and the open door, turned to her. "What is it? What's wrong?"

Ji-Min grabbed for him, but Jamie twisted out of the way, then scrambled into the car and across the front seat. "Open. Please open. Doesn't this door work anymore?" He thrust the weight of his body against the driver's-side door, but he couldn't make it move. What was Cicely screaming about? Why wasn't Louise helping her? He crawled into the backseat before remembering that those doors didn't open either.

Ji-Min had blocked the one open door, and Jamie rummaged around looking for something to throw at him.

Ji-Min snarled, "There's nothing there. I looked through everything earlier."

So that's who'd gone through the car. Jamie squirmed, and the weight of the forgotten stone fell against his thigh. Shielding his movements from Ji-Min with the bag of chocolate, Jamie flung the rock at the window.

Most of the broken glass, pulled by the force of the blow, fell on the ground, but a single large shard glanced against his cheek. Jamie reached up and felt the sticky blood. "Not bad, it's not too bad," he muttered, scrambling through the opening. He hit the dirt, skidding on the rubble. He tightened his grip on the chocolate. "I'm sorry about the window, Louise! I'm sor—"

Jamie stopped short. Cicely was sobbing now. Her hands, which she held over her face, muffled the sounds. It must be her eyes and not her mouth she's trying to cover, thought Jamie. He would have done the same had he not been frozen. Where Louise had been, there now stood a sleek brown wolf. And as Jamie watched, the wolf turned a familiar golden gaze toward him.

"Louise," he said, after a pause. There was no uncertainty in his voice. "It's Louise, isn't it?" He looked at Cicely. She was crying too hard to answer.

"Well, you finally figured it out."

Jamie had forgotten all about Ji-Min, but turned on him

now with a sudden fury. "What have you done to her? How could you do this?"

"It's what she wanted. Don't be so quick to judge. Try to understand."

"What are you talking about?" Jamie raged at his uncle. He turned to Cicely and shouted, "What's he talking about? What's he done?"

"Go ahead and tell him, Cicely. Maybe he'll believe you."

"It's what she wanted once, maybe, but not like this, Ji-Min. Not like this."

"There is no other way. We're running out of time. It had to be now if she was going to travel with the pack this year. It's going to be an early winter, and a hard one. She knew that, but she wouldn't push him. It has to be now. We have to leave now, and we have to leave together. I can't leave her behind. I won't go without her again." Jamie could see his uncle struggling to stay calm.

"I know," said Cicely weakly. "But, well, Louise said that maybe I could . . ."

"Could what?" The man's voice had risen slightly. He took a single step toward the girl.

"Nothing," she said. "You're right. This is what Louise said she wanted."

Jamie noticed the slight emphasis on the word *said*. He tried to catch Cicely's eye, but she looked away.

"Are you ready to play?" Ji-Min's voice was barely audible.

Cicely held out her hand without looking at him. He passed her the wolf whistle.

She lifted the flute to her lips. "Wait," said Ji-Min. He turned to Jamie. "After she's done, it's your turn. Do you remember the music you played the night we met? Can you still play it?"

Jamie nodded slowly. Of course he remembered how to play it. That didn't mean he would.

Ji-Min narrowed his eyes at his nephew. "It's Cicely's music. The music that will shift her. And if you don't play it right, and all the way through, you'll be sorry. That goes for both of you."

Jamie reached up and unconsciously rubbed the wound on his cheek, causing it to bleed again. He looked at the fresh blood on his fingers and knew his uncle could, and would, do worse. Jamie nodded. "I understand."

The brown wolf—Louise, Jamie reminded himself—had been pacing near them. She growled softly and flicked her ears back. She was clearly agitated, but Jamie couldn't tell if it was because of his uncle's insistence or his own reluctance to comply. Now he turned to Cicely. "Does she know what we're saying?"

His uncle snorted. "What difference does it make? I told you—"

"I'm not talking to you." Jamie flung the bag of chocolate to the ground. "Does she?"

"Yes, sort of." After a pause, Cicely continued. "It's different, though. Pictures rather than words, and not everything. At least not for me." She added this last bit hastily, after a slightly louder growl from Louise.

Jamie nodded, then turned to the wolf. "Louise," he began hesitantly, but his voice grew stronger as he continued. "Louise, what should I do?"

"She's not going to talk!" Ji-Min jabbed his fist in the air. "And what difference does it make? I've told you, you have to play."

"And I told you I understand what you mean. But my dad told me to trust Louise." Jamie's voice was firm.

"Your dad? Where is he?" shouted Ji-Min. "He left. I trained him for this, and he left."

"Better do it, Jamie. Better do it now." Cicely's voice was low and sad.

"Are you sure?"

She nodded but didn't look him in the eye.

"Louise," Jamie said again, "what should I do?" He watched the wolf carefully. If she understood in pictures, would she speak to him in pictures? He waited a moment, but all he could think of was the long-ago conversation with his mother. *Guard the small green shoot.* As he remembered the words, he pictured one of the plants in Louise's garden, but that had to be a coincidence. He sighed and turned to Ji-Min.

"Okay, tell me what to do."

"Cicely plays first. And then you—*exactly* the way you did that night."

Jamie nodded grimly.

The wolf began pacing again. The girl began to play the flute. Jamie wanted to cry. It was the melody Louise had played with him the night Ji-Min and Cicely had stepped into the cabin. Jamie felt the tears come to his eyes. Cicely was a much better musician than Louise. The music was beautiful. She finished playing and held out the flute to him.

Jamie heard the raspy breathing of a second wolf behind him. "What happened?"

"Just what it sounds like." Cicely's voice was barely audible. "Don't look."

He took the flute and ran his fingers over the marks carved in the bone. As he did so, he noticed that the fine hairs on his arm were sticking straight up. He glanced at Louise. She stopped pacing and stared back. Again he pictured something small growing in her garden. "I still don't get it," he said. She circled as Jamie began to play.

He was nearly at the end of the sequence when he once more pictured Louise's garden. Now the plant was bent over, its leaves wilted and brown around the edges. *Guard the small green shoot.* Suddenly it made sense! He recognized the plant: sweet cicely, one of the medicinals his aunt grew. Of course, he hadn't made the connection before, but if Louise was thinking in pictures, that meant . . . His playing faded and then stopped.

Ji-Min growled behind him. Cicely looked up. "You didn't finish."

"I know. I'm not going to. Louise doesn't think I should."

He felt rather than heard his uncle leap at him. Jamie quickly crouched down and picked up the bag of chocolate. He spun on his heel as he stood, and had just a moment to notice how magnificent the enormous black wolf was before the sack crashed into his forelegs. "Run, Cicely, run," he shouted. Ji-Min staggered, then quickly regained his balance. He took a step after the fleeing girl but turned back to his nephew with a snarl.

Jamie swung the bag again. Out of the corner of his eye he saw Louise advancing. He was afraid that they would both attack him, but she lunged at Ji-Min, her jaws fixing in the ruff of dark fur across his back. Jamie edged nearer to the path, then hesitated. He didn't want Louise to get hurt. But Ji-Min shook her off and turned on Jamie. She reared, then pounced a second time. Jamie ran toward the cabin, clutching the chocolate in one hand and Ji-Min's flute in the other.

Gus was crowing loudly as Jamie entered the clearing. Jamie heard the panting and snorting drawing closer. He slowed slightly when he hit the steps of the cabin and rammed the door open with his shoulder. He flung the sack to the floor, but something grabbed his leg when he tried to follow. Jamie turned and saw a black muzzle clamped around his calf. An instant later Louise ran into the clearing and lunged. Jamie heard a ripping sound as she hit. The force of the impact loosened his uncle's grip. Jamie broke free, jumped inside, and thrust the door shut behind him. He dropped the large wooden latch, fell against the wall, and watched his blood spread across the floor.

"Dad. *Ah-ba!*"

*Wild
Mushroom*

CHAPTER II

*EDITOR'S NOTE: Some scholars, includ-
ing the noted linguist Carolyn J. Park, dis-
agree with Park Dai-Jeong's interpretation of
the marks carved on the flutes. Her opposing
theory is set forth in the article "Ancient
System of Musical Notation Differs Greatly
from Western Staves Form."*
—The Journal of Applied Linguistics,
Vol. XXIV, No.7

Jamie had been rereading his father's articles trying to find
information about the flutes. He was hoping to discover what

made them work. And once he found out, he would know how to make Louise Louise again. He skimmed over the footnote. If he hadn't been so nervous, he would have (as he usually did with small print of any kind) skipped it altogether, but reading kept him from worrying about everything else.

His leg was swollen and festered; he tried to stay off it as much as possible. Even if he could have moved easily, he was still trapped in the cabin. Ji-Min had prowled the clearing for three days, occasionally growling at the door. Yesterday his fangs had just missed Jamie's arm when, thinking the coast was clear, Jamie leaned out the door to empty the basin he'd been using as a chamber pot.

Now he scrunched his back against the wall and stretched his leg out along the full length of Louise's bed. He jammed a couple of pillows under his thigh, elevating the injured calf, and looked out the window. The black wolf stared back from the shadows. Jamie shook his head and kept reading.

"*Carolyn J. Park.*" The same name as my mother, he thought. "*. . . the noted linguist . . .*" That *is* my mother! Jamie forgot the pain in his leg as he read the footnote again. His mother disagreed with his father, and she'd written an article about it. That was not that unusual. They had loved to argue about their research, bouncing ideas and theories off each other with the excitement everyone else he knew reserved for a soccer match.

Jamie checked the date of the journal. It had been published just about the time his parents had stopped coming here to visit. And that, at least according to Louise and Ji-Min, had been his mother's decision. Why? What had she discovered?

He whipped through the stack of magazines hoping to find his mother's article—no luck. His leg had started to throb again. The edge of the wound was turning green, and the red lines that spidered out from the torn flesh had begun to crawl higher on his leg. Jamie tried to remember what he'd learned about infections in health class. He didn't think this was a good sign.

He eased himself off the bed and hobbled over to the woodstove, bracing himself against the wall as he opened the door and threw in a few logs. Back in bed, he studied the note again, but he couldn't focus. "Later, Mom," he said. "Now I have to take a nap."

When he woke, he heard the sound of embers settling in the woodstove. Their faint glow was the only light in the cabin, and the room was cold. Jamie looked through the stove's window and knew he would have to put more wood in soon or he'd lose the fire. Despite Louise's thorough coaching, he wasn't sure he could start it up again from scratch. He hauled himself off the bed with difficulty and limped toward the stove. His leg felt worse.

The logs piled in the corner were already cut to size; it took only a few minutes for them to ignite. As flames brightened the room, he held his hands out to catch the warmth. He remembered bristling at his aunt's exacting instructions about the correct way to split this wood, but now—he sucked a mouthful of air through his teeth in response to the pain in his leg—he wondered what would have happened to him without her vigilant preparations.

Wood; water; food. He figured if he was careful, his supplies would last another two or three days. Then what? Jamie shook his head. Even if he felt strong enough to follow the path to the dirt road—which he didn't—he had no idea where he was or what direction to go. He could refill the buckets at the pump, and he figured even smoked trout would taste pretty good if he were hungry enough, but it wouldn't last forever either. And then there was the small matter of dodging his four-footed uncle. Jamie looked out into the dark clearing and shuddered.

The candles from Louise's last trip to the market still lay on the table. Jamie lit one now and held it near his leg. He probed the wound with his free hand. The skin was hot, and the whole leg was tender. He found a holder for the candle and, in its flickering light, scanned the bundles of herbs hanging from the ceiling. What had Louise mixed with the beeswax? Garlic, he thought. Chamomile. And goldenseal. He steeped the herbs in boiling water, then threw one of his old T-shirts in the pot. When it had cooled, he pulled it out and wrapped it around his leg.

He was too sick to eat, but forced some water between his fever-cracked lips before going back to bed. At the back

of his mind, he was dimly aware that something else needed
to be done, something with the flutes, he thought. But sleep
and fevered dreams came before he could figure out what
it was.

Gus was crowing. He had been for some time. Jamie
opened his eyes. It was not quite light outside. "Show some
consideration," he mumbled, and rolled over. Gus started to
shriek. Jamie sat up. The rooster should still have food and
water, but although Gus had complained loudly over the past
days, he now sounded frantic. Jamie pushed to his feet and,
after wrapping a quilt around himself, went to the front window. Ji-Min was on his hind paws, his forelegs against the door
of the coop, his nose pushing against the latch.

Jamie opened the door. "Get away," he cried, his concern
for the rooster overcoming his own fear and pain. Ji-Min
dropped to the ground and looked back over his shoulder at
Jamie. His eyes were dull, as was the once-shiny ruff of fur
across his back. Jamie noticed a sharpness in the line of ribs
that ran from haunch to shoulder blade. Their eyes met briefly
before the wolf limped off to the shelter of bracken at the edge
of the clearing. Hungry and injured, thought Jamie, just like
me. Compassion for his uncle mingled with anger and fear.

He turned back into the cabin. Two of his four water
buckets were empty. Without waiting to change his mind,
he hoisted a full pail to his good hip. Walking carefully, he
stepped out onto the landing and placed the bucket down.

"Here, Ji-Min," he called. "And the trout is still in the smokehouse. After all, you are my uncle."

The wolf stood and walked toward the cabin. After he'd covered about half the distance, he stopped and stared at his nephew. His eyes held respect and concern—but his body was taut and his tail twitched. He feels like I do, thought Jamie. As the wolf mounted the step, Jamie quickly stepped inside and barred the door.

Jamie fought the urge to go back to bed. It seemed that he was not the only one trapped here: Gus in the henhouse; Ji-Min in the clearing; the rest of his pack in the woods somewhere, waiting to move to their winter home; and Cicely—what of her? Jamie pushed his hair back behind his ears, then walked to the table and picked up a worn strip of leather. He drew it taut between his fingers and gave it a tug so that it twanged slightly. He heard something climb the step outside, and then the sound of water sloshing. "It looks like it all depends on me, doesn't it?" Jamie turned toward the closed door. "Give me your strength, Ji-Min, and your courage," he said as he tied back his hair.

He cleared the table then. Later it would hold a candle and a cup of coffee, and the floor would be littered with crumpled paper. But he started with it empty. After wiping it clean with another of his old T-shirts (Louise had traded him a single flannel shirt for all his ripped garments; she needed rags, he just needed something to wear), he laid out the magazine that mentioned his mother's article. Next to it he put the flutes: Louise's, his own (this one he cradled gently in his hand before setting it down), Ji-Min's (quickly dropped), and the broken one he'd uncovered on the mountain. He found some paper and three pencils without points, which he carefully sharpened using a small knife. These, too, he laid on the table before he sat down and began to write.

WHAT I KNOW

1. *The flute music changes people into wolves and wolves into people.*

His hand shook as he put down the pencil. After a moment, he picked it up and started writing again.

2. *Everybody (at least everybody who can shift; I don't think everybody can) has music that changes only them.*
3. *I know the music for Cicely, but I'm not going to play it.*
4. *I heard Louise's, but I can't remember it.*
5. *I know some of Ji-Min's, but not all of it.*
6. *I think people can play their own music and shift; but once they become wolves, they can't play the flute and shift back.*
7. *Without me, or someone else who knows*

> *how, to play the flute and make them*
> *human again, the three of them cannot be*
> *wolves at the same time.*

And that's what Ji-Min wants, thought Jamie, for the three of them to be wolves at the same time. He rubbed his leg. It still hurt but wasn't quite as tender. He peeled off the cloths he'd used as bandages. The swelling was down, and the red lines had receded. Garlic and herbs, he thought. I need to bring Louise back if only to thank her. He stood up, paced the room, opened cupboards and drawers, ate a few chocolate chips, and poured the chips left in the bag onto the corner of the table. He sat back down.

WHAT I DON'T KNOW
1. *Just about everything else.*

Jamie got up, opened all the same cupboards and draw-ers, put a log in the fire, filled a glass with water, drank it, and sat back down.

He pushed the first piece of paper off to one side, ate a few chips, took a fresh sheet, and wrote: *Ancient System of Musical Notation.* He checked the magazine to be sure he'd spelled everything right, underlined the words, ate a few more chips. His dad thought the little designs were decoration. His mom thought they were like notes, that they represented sounds.

She was probably right. She certainly played these flutes often enough in the weeks before she died.

He picked up Louise's flute: five holes. With the tip of his pencil he poked Ji-Min's instrument: five holes. He grabbed it as it started to roll off the table. He studied the broken flute: only four. He rubbed the small notch at the cracked end, then tilted the whistle to catch the midday light. There could have been more once. He knew how many holes his own flute had, but he picked it up anyway. Five.

He continued to hold the polished length of bone as he examined the designs. Each was made with a short vertical line—with dots on it, or sometimes little horizontal hatch marks.

He ran his index finger over the marks. The dots felt as though they'd been punched in by a pointed awl. But the lines were shaped like valleys—they must have been carved with some kind of tiny beveled chisel. Two separate tools: a lot of work for something that was just decoration.

The designs looked like a game from the back of a cereal box: Find the one that's different. Jamie grinned. He loved those puzzles. "Mmmm, cereal would be good." He reached for the pile of chips and realized he'd eaten them all. His stomach rumbled. "I'll take a break and make some tea when I've finished this," he said to himself. "It'll be nice to have something to look forward to." Carefully, he began to compare the flutes.

The sun was shining in the opposite side of the cabin by the time he had finished. He studied the notes he had made. No line had more than five marks on it, most had fewer. Five marks; five holes in the flutes. "Now we're getting somewhere. This'll be a piece of cake. Cake! Oh man, I'm really hungry." Jamie's words were not as loud as his protesting stomach. "Okay, okay," he said as he rubbed his ribs. "Let's see what we can find to eat."

Jamie pushed himself up from the table. His leg had started to throb again. He forced himself to peel more garlic cloves, and to add them, along with a handful of herbs, to the pot on the woodstove.

While this potion simmered, Jamie made another tour of the room. Cupboards, nothing. Drawers, nothing. He'd used the last of the flour and honey yesterday, the end of the rice the day before that. He couldn't get to the foods Louise had put away for winter without going outside; it had all been stored in the cool depths of the root cellar. Everything else his aunt ate came fresh from the field, forest, or garden: eggs, goat milk, berries and tomatoes, fish, game.

He fingered the bunches of herbs that hung from the rafters and decided he couldn't face another cup of tea. It reminded him too much of the stuff he was putting on his leg. That left . . . "Coffee," Jamie sighed. He filled the hopper of Louise's hand-cranked grinder with beans and turned the cast-iron handle. The ground coffee settled into the wooden base of the mill, and its dark smell wafted through the cabin. He put the teakettle on the woodstove and set the herbs aside to cool.

The wind had been building all afternoon. Now, with the sun low in the sky, the cabin felt cold. He stood close to the stove while he waited for the water to boil. As he reached out to grab the whistling kettle, his hand grazed its surface. He pulled back quickly with a grunt of surprise. It's like Ji-Min, he thought, sucking his burned fingers. Warm and inviting—but dangerous if you get too close.

As if in response to these thoughts, Jamie heard the door rattle and something plop on the steps. He looked out the front window. Ji-Min was halfway across the clearing, heading toward the woods. His belly was distended, so swollen in fact that it rubbed against the scrubby grass. He turned, looked at Jamie, licked his lips. Jamie could swear that he grinned. When the wolf settled into the shadows, Jamie opened the door a crack. Two smoked trout lay on the landing. Two and a half if you counted the one with a bite out of it.

"I guess I'm not worth much to you if I starve, am I?" He considered the situation for only a moment before grabbing all three fish. He nodded at his uncle. "Thank you," he whispered, and stepped back inside.

Jamie wiped the dirt away with the dampened corner of an old shirt before placing the trout on Louise's favorite plate. He got a knife and fork. And a napkin. He made coffee, filled a mug, and sat down on the floor near the the stove. He made himself cut the fish into small pieces, and chewed each bite slowly. His next meal? Who knew? And anyway (he hunched protectively over the food) wolfing it down seemed a little too close to home.

When he was done, Jamie threw the bones into the fire. He used the damp shirt to wipe his hands, then checked his leg. It still hurt, but it looked better. He picked up the untouched coffee and put it on the corner of the table. The smell reminded him of Louise. He sat down and adjusted his papers, fiddled with a pencil, moved the coffee mug closer to the center of the table. He laid the pencil down and picked up his flute.

Without really thinking, Jamie began to play. His fingers whipped over the holes. It wasn't Cicely's music, or Ji-Min's, or anything else that Louise had taught him. He made it up as he went along. When he was done, he eyed the instrument curiously for a long time. "Like the fire and Ji-Min," he said at last. "Beautiful and dangerous."

It surprised him that he wasn't more alarmed by the strangeness of the situation. He was worried about his leg, and nervous about his lack of food. But the fact that his vision of reality had been so radically altered hardly bothered him at all. In truth, he admitted to himself, it was almost a relief to have his suspicions about the wolves confirmed. Otherwise nothing that had happened during the summer made sense.

He studied the designs again, trying to decipher their

meaning. They reminded him of Hangul, the Korean alphabet. Or maybe more like pictographs. The vertical lines looked a little like flutes, and the hatch marks—Jamie began to get excited—the hatch marks looked like fingers. "And the dot must be for the little hole on the bottom of the flute."

It seemed too easy. For a moment or so he tried to convince himself that he couldn't be right. Then he decided to assume he was. Why not? After all, if the marks were meant to transcribe music (as his mother thought), the easier the better as far as Jamie was concerned.

He fooled around with the finger combinations for quite a while, trying to decide if the marks represented covered or uncovered holes. It was nearly dark before he was satisfied with his arrangement. He stood and stretched, then lit the last of Louise's beeswax candles. He sat back down and picked up his flute. He wanted to practice playing something.

He looked at the other three flutes. The marks on the old flute were too worn to decipher. Jamie had never liked Ji-Min's flute—he didn't want anything to do with it. He shuddered as he pushed it aside. That left Louise's. He picked it up. Parts of its design were worn too. He could read the marks off his own instrument and play hers, but he felt uncomfortable doing that—she didn't even like to have him touch her flute. No, thought Jamie, that won't work either.

At last he decided, despite the extra time it would take, to copy the marks from his own flute onto a sheet of paper and play from that. He moved the candle closer—it was already burning low—and began to copy the designs. Something about these marks, their sequence, seemed very familiar. Jamie paused at one point and flexed his fingers, his eye roving over the carefully inked images. "Wow," he whispered, tracing them with his finger.

Fatigue and pain hampered his movements, but eventually he made it up the ladder to his loft. It was too dark to see, but he knew what he was after. He groped around for the wooden box and pulled from its lacquered interior the letter from his father. Jamie eased himself back onto the ladder. Getting down was harder. He couldn't believe he had leaped from these rungs so carelessly, and not so long ago; he hardly remembered who he had been then.

He didn't even wait to sit down before unfolding the piece of notepaper. He spread it out under the candle's flickering light. The designs matched the marks on the flute. Exactly.

Why? What did it mean?

Tentatively he played the first few notes. He forgot his questions. The music made him feel wild and free. It made him feel like himself. He missed a note.

He started the sequence over again, from the beginning. It was the way Louise made him do it in practice. "Don't finish till it's perfect." He could almost hear her. He made another mistake. He was panting slightly.

Over and over, he tried to get through the complicated sequences and tricky fingering. He wasn't tired anymore, or hungry. He was not aware of the passing of time, nor of the steady gathering of wolves in the clearing.

He was nearly through now. Two more notes. One. The candle sputtered and went out. Jamie hadn't finished playing. But he had, after all his practice, committed the sequence to memory. He started to play it again, but stopped. "Not in the dark," he whispered. "I don't want to end in the dark." He put his head down on the table. Later, he fell asleep.

He woke as he had when he was younger—dimly aware for a time that he was being called, but unable to make his muscles move or his voice cry out. The room was still black. Something was wrong. Jamie pushed himself to his feet. He had held the flute while he slept, and now he brandished it in front of his chest. He raised it to the height of his shoulder and angled it down, instinctively holding it as one might hold a dagger. Awkwardly, still clumsy with sleep, he patrolled the room, his injured leg dragging.

He checked the door, then glanced out the front window. His eyes had adjusted to the dark. The clearing, high-lighted by the moon's milky light, appeared empty. Trees bordering its edges shadowed the packed earth and the gardens. Jamie could make out the pump, the outhouse, and the coop where Gus slept quietly. He was about to turn around, thinking to stretch out on Louise's bed, when something pulled his gaze back to the clearing.

Off to the side, at the point where the path from the road entered the yard, there was a momentary thickening of the darkness. Then a form broke free of the shadows and stepped into the clearing. Neither Louise nor Cicely, thought Jamie. Ji-Min? Maybe, although this person (Jamie decided it was a man) moved tentatively, without Ji-Min's grace and confidence. The figure stumbled and reached for his face with a motion that reminded Jamie of the way his father straightened his glasses.

"Dad!" Jamie burst through the door of the cabin waving the flute in the air, the pain in his leg no match for his relief. But before he could reach his father, or even call to him again, someone else was there. The newcomer's snarled greeting caused Jamie's own to catch in his throat.

Ji-Min stood between father and son, eyes glinting and teeth shining in the darkness. His black form moved with the shadows. It was hard to tell where wolf left off and night began. To Jamie, who was weak with pain and hunger, his uncle appeared formidable. He glanced at his father, who wore, as usual, a short-sleeved white shirt. Jamie could tell there was a pen in the pocket, because, like Ji-Min's eyes, it reflected the moonlight. His father's glasses were crooked. This is going to be a slam dunk, thought Jamie.

"What did you say?" His father smiled shyly. "You have grown so tall." Dai-Jeong held out his arms and took a step toward Jamie. The wolf rose slightly on his hind legs. "And you, brother." Dai-Jeong pushed his glasses up on his nose. "It has been a long time since we've seen each other."

Ji-Min growled.

"So be it." Dai-Jeong appeared totally unruffled. "You'll excuse us, then. I've come to take Jamie home."

"Uh, Dad. *Ah-ba.*"

His father grinned. "It is so good to see you, Jamie."

"Yeah, you too. But Dad, there's a problem."

"You're not ready to go?" His father tried again to straighten his glasses.

"Well, actually, I'd love to go. I've got a pretty bad cut on my leg and I . . ." Jamie's eyes had gotten used to the darkness, and he noticed for the first time that a number of wolves— four? five?—stood or sat around the clearing. Not much chance of escape. Jamie studied the shapes, trying to decide if they included his aunt or Cicely.

Ji-Min growled again, pulling back his lips.

"Dad, he's not going to let me go. . . ."

"What? Why not?" Dai-Jeong looked at his brother. "Ahh. It's about the girl, is it?" He paused. Ji-Min swished his tail. "No, not wolf. Girl. And that is her choice, is it not? Louise wrote that Cicely wishes to winter with us."

Jamie spotted them, standing apart from the others. Cicely's long hair was loose, and her hand rested on the broad plain of fur at the base of Louise's neck.

"Come, Jamie." He followed his son's gaze. "Shall we take her with us?"

With that, Ji-Min lunged. Dai-Jeong stumbled but kept his balance. Jamie saw him reach toward his face, not for the glasses this time, but for his cheek. Even in the moonlight Jamie could make out the dark gash that ran from his father's temple to his jaw. The wolf jumped again, this time pinning the man to the ground.

"Dad!" Jamie bolted, ignoring the pain in his leg.

Cicely ran into the clearing. "No, Jamie, don't." She sounded hysterical. "He'll kill him. Play. You have to play the flute. There's no other way."

Jamie watched her. She was absolutely right. He had no choice. Why hadn't he thought of it sooner? Moving quickly, he brought the flute to his lips. He took a deep breath and began. His eyes were closed. He was afraid that if he watched his dad struggle—or worse, if his dad ceased to struggle—he would play too fast and make a mistake. And there wasn't time for mistakes.

Near the end, he grew nervous. He wasn't sure he remembered the final notes. He wanted to stop. His arms felt funny, as though they couldn't hold the flute any longer. He opened his eyes and saw Louise watching him. She had left the shelter of the woods and again stood at Cicely's side.

Her steady gaze kept him going. He ignored everything else. When he had at last completed the music, he dropped to the ground. Only then did he look at Cicely, at her fingers twined in Louise's fur. "That's not what I meant," she whispered as she reached for the discarded flute.

But Jamie had already turned. He started running. Two graceful leaps and his jaws were clamped on Ji-Min's haunch. The older wolf reared in surprise, then shook free. Jamie pounced again, raking his claws across the furry back.

His uncle turned on him, ramming against his ribs. Jamie flinched at the impact. He circled and backed up slightly, just out of striking distance.

What next? He sniffed. The air was moist, acrid. It smelled like something. He groped for words. There were no words. He tried again to place the smell. Fear. He felt the guard hairs stiffen on either side of his spine. Fear. But not his.

Jamie charged. He grabbed his uncle's throat. Ji-Min tried to pull away but couldn't throw him off. Jamie tightened his jaws and dug his hind claws into the ground.

Ji-Min's breath was labored. A low strangled cry shook his body. Jamie hesitated. What next? There were no words. He pictured a man sitting on the step of the cabin eating pancakes. He saw him bending down to pick up cherries from the floor. Jamie loosened his grip. Finally a word came to him. One word. *Family*. He let go of his uncle.

Dai-Jeong lay on the ground, moaning. Louise had trotted to him, ready to protect him from another assault. But it wasn't really necessary.

The older wolf was weakened by thirst and hunger, his movements slowed by a belly full of fish. He limped badly, and his fur was matted with blood. Ji-Min whimpered as he turned toward the mountain. Jamie watched him go. Louise growled at the pack hiding in the trees. They cowered and whined, then melted back into the woods with their tails low.

That left just the four of them: a girl with a flute, an injured man, and two wolves.

Sorrel

CHAPTER 12

It is not enough to believe what you see. You
must also understand what you see.
—*Leonardo da Vinci*

Madame Mahoney was lecturing the class on the proper use
of the imperfect tense.

Jamie wasn't paying attention. He stared at the words written on the blackboard—they reminded him of something. He
turned in his chair, carefully easing his injured leg out into
the aisle between the desks. The wound, though almost
healed, was still sore, and he didn't want to risk banging it
before the coming afternoon's race.

He read the words again and remembered where he had heard them before: His father had said almost the same thing to him on the car ride home from the cabin. Jamie had asked why he had heard the wolves for months before he saw them.

"These animals have become very good at hiding in the world of men. My brother . . ." Dai-Jeong stopped talking.

"It's okay, Dad," Jamie said softly. "I still love him too. It's strange, but I actually feel closer to him now. I feel like I know why he acted the way he did."

Dai-Jeong gave Jamie a long, thoughtful look before turning his gaze back to the road. "My brother says that there are many more of these creatures than we are aware of, and that the world is much more mysterious than we realize." Dai-Jeong turned the wheel quickly, and the car veered around a turtle crossing the road. "I think that what is unusual or unexpected can be right before our eyes without us seeing it. Not because it's invisible—but because if we don't understand what we see, we don't believe what we see. Like a research question: The answer is there all along, but until I can imagine it, I can't know it. I read once that it is imagination that gives shape to the universe."

"That makes sense," Jamie said. "I guess."

"Spoken like a scientist. Your mom would be pleased." Dai-Jeong glanced at his son. The flute and a few notebooks rested in the boy's lap. "She'd be very pleased, Jamie," he added in a softer voice.

"Dad, did she know about Louise and Ji-Min? About the wolf part, I mean?"

His father nodded, but it was a long time before he replied. "Yes. Even before I did. The four of us were very close for a while. But when my brother . . ." His voice faded.

"Go ahead. Tell me."

"We used to bring you to the cabin." His father glanced at Jamie.

"I know, Louise told me."

"Well, once Ji-Min tried . . . he played the flute, your music I think, although I didn't realize it at the time. But somehow your mother knew. She began to run as he played, then swooped you up in her arms without missing a step, and kept running until she was at the car. She refused to go back. Ever. At the time I was so angry with her." Dai-Jeong clenched the steering wheel and his jaw tightened. "But later I saw she was trying to protect you. Not so much from the possibility of shape-shifting—she understood that—but from having that life forced on you without your choosing it."

"Like what happened to Cicely."

"Yes, like Cicely."

The car bumped along the dirt road. "Dad, where is she?"

"Cicely? I don't know." His father shook his head. "It happened so quickly. She played the flute and changed you back. She must have learned the melody from Ji-Min, although I don't think she realized what it was until she heard you play it. As soon as she'd finished, she dropped your flute and ran into the woods. Louise trotted after her. I was on my feet by then, but still bleeding badly. I couldn't move fast enough to stop them. And I was afraid to leave you. You were crumpled on the ground, and your leg . . ." His father shuddered.

"Not to mention your face." Jamie tried to make a joke of it. "You're going to have a wicked scar."

"Yes, it does hurt," said his father, matching Jamie's light tone. "But I think the scar will look dashing, don't you?" He turned and smiled at his son. The car swerved, hitting a deep rut along the side of the road. Gus complained loudly from the backseat. "Couldn't you have stayed with rocks?" Dai-Jeong looked at the reflection of the scruffy rooster in the rearview mirror.

"He's great. You'll learn to love him. Really." They were quiet for a while. Dai-Jeong kept his eyes on the road. Jamie looked out the back window at the line of mountains fading behind him. "Dad." Jamie turned forward. "Do you know the music too? Is that why you put the marks on the bottom of your letters?"

"Is that how you learned it?" His father shook his head in surprise. "I wondered. I can play the flutes a little—but I had no idea what those marks meant. Your mother had them written on a sheet of paper that I found pinned to the wall of her workroom. At the top she'd written: *For Jamie when he leaves.*

I had no idea what she meant, but I felt I owed it to both of you to make sure you had them."

"How did Mom learn to read them?"

Dai-Jeong shook his head. "I'm not sure. I know she was working with the melodies before she died. But my guess is that Cicely's father told her sometime before that. They were friends." He glanced at his son. "He was a flute maker."

"Monsieur Park." A stern voice interrupted Jamie's reverie. "Would you like to tell us what is so much more compelling than this lesson?" Madame Mahoney tapped her right foot on the floor.

She must have gotten those shoes in Paris, thought Jamie. They were the same color red as her hair.

"Monsieur Park!" Her voice had risen an octave.

He looked at her and swallowed. "I was reading what was on the blackboard," he finally answered, pointing in that general direction.

"I have not been writing on the board during class today."

"No. I mean, yes." He gestured to the board again.

She turned and read the words written there, then glared at Jamie. "You will stay after class," she said as the bell rang.

Madame Mahoney sat down at her desk. His classmates rushed out into the hallway. Jamie slunk to the front of the room.

"So." She pointed her pencil at him. "You like da Vinci?"

Jamie nodded. "But he's not French, is he? I thought he was Italian."

"You're right. A Renaissance artist and scientist. Would you like me to write the quote down for you?" She didn't wait for him to respond and, in a moment, handed him a slip of paper. "I've written down your homework assignment as well. I expect it to be completed by tomorrow or your grade will drop. No excuses. Now, you'd better hurry. You have a race, no?"

"Yes." He grinned. "Madame Mahoney?"

She looked up from her work.

"Thanks for yelling at me."

She arched an eyebrow at him, then shook her head. "I think I know what you mean, but let's not do it again."

By the time Jamie changed and ran out to the field, the girls had already started racing. He could see them disappearing into the woods, the bottoms of their shoes flicking against the dark line of trees like the tails of the deer that ran wild at Louise's. Jamie tried to push thoughts of the cabin out of his mind. He didn't want to think about how happy he'd been there, or of how much he missed Louise and Cicely. Can't be sad when I run, he thought as he stretched, carefully testing the flexibility of his injured leg. Can't be distracted.

He turned to the crowd, searching for his father. Dai-Jeong had come to a number of practices, and Jamie really wanted him to see this first race. Yesterday morning, however, his dad had left town early, telling Jamie only that he had to be gone overnight on unexpected business, and that he would try to be back in time for the meet. He'd wanted Jamie to stay with the neighbors. But Jamie had pointed out that the neighbors would not want to mess with Gus, and for that matter, neither would anyone else—the rooster was better protection than any guard dog. Not, thought Jamie, that he really needed guarding anymore after what he'd been through, but he decided not to point this out to his father.

He scanned the crowd again. Last spring his father's absence would have upset Jamie, but now he felt certain that his father would make it if he could. He finally spotted him, standing alone at the edge of the group of spectators. Dai-Jeong wore, as usual, a white shirt and a tie. His dad had been right—the scar was dashing. A couple of mothers wandered over to his father and started talking. Dai-Jeong caught Jamie's eye and waved.

Jamie trotted over to join his teammates. They stood around the starting line in small groups. Some were stretching, others watching the competition. Most were chatting and laughing. Jamie tightened the strip of leather that held back his hair, half listening to the conversation.

"Where did she come from?"

"I don't know. But she's really fast."

"What do you think, Jamie?" One of the boys nudged his foot. "Could she beat you?"

"What?" Jamie looked up.

"The new girl. She started today, and she's already running cross-country. Didn't you see her?"

He shook his head.

"Well, you must be the only one who didn't. Come on, it's time to start."

Jamie began to run, and the grunts and gasps of the other racers faded into the background. Only the thud of his foot-falls broke the stillness of the afternoon. His right leg hit with a solid thwack, his injured left leg with a softer sound, drag-ging slightly through the fallen leaves. He corrected his stride. He wondered if the wolves would come. Then he realized that they wouldn't: not to this race, not to any of the others.

He slowed, then stopped. The other kids pounded by. Jamie watched their bright jerseys slicing through the woods. The wolves might not come, but he could try to find them. And if he found them, he had the flute. Jamie began to move, passing one group of runners, then another, propelled by rhythms that he alone could hear. He wasn't first across the line, but it didn't matter. The race didn't matter. His father looked across at him and smiled.

A few of his teammates called, "What happened?"

Jamie shrugged, then pointed to his ankle. He felt some-thing brush against the backs of his legs. I'm imagining things, he thought, imagining the wolves are back.

He started to walk toward the locker rooms. Something

grabbed at his elbow. He kept walking. Suddenly he felt a leg hook around his and trip him. He fell, then scrambled to his feet and turned to glare.

"Jamie," she said, "why are you ignoring me?"

"Cicely? Cicely! What are you doing here?"

"I'm going to school." She gave him an exasperated look. "It's fun, except for the cafeteria."

"I know what you mean," he replied. "The kids eat like animals."

"You should know." Her mouth twitched.

"Yeah, I guess so." Jamie grinned. "How did you get here?"

"Your dad came for me. I like him. Tomorrow he's going to make mandoo, those dumplings you were always talking about."

Jamie nodded. "Tomorrow is Chusok, the Korean harvest feast. We've been planning the menu for weeks. But how did he know where to find you?"

"He left me a note at the cabin with his phone number. And Louise taught me how to use a telephone the last time we were at the market. They both knew I wanted to come here. To try this life. Louise said it would be better if I knew both ways . . ." Cicely's voice faded.

"I miss her too."

Cicely nodded. "Here, I'll show you Dai-Jeong's letter." She rummaged through the pockets of her shorts, and bits of paper blew free and were gathered up by the breeze.

"You ran with all that in your pockets?" He tried not to laugh.

"How else do you keep track of everything here?"

"I'll help, don't worry," said Jamie as he bent to collect the loose papers. "But I don't think you'll have any problems," he added, handing her the letter.

"Dear Cicely," she read out loud:

> *"You will find my office telephone number at the bottom of this note. I am sure you do not remember me, but we were very close when you were young. Louise tells me you are a quick learner, and that you picked up English easily. Perhaps you would like to study Korean? Here is a start:* Sa rang hae yo. *I used to say it to you often. I will tell you what it means when you call.*
>
> *"Park Dai-Jeong"*

"What *does* it mean, Jamie? He didn't tell me."

"*Sa rang hae yo?*" He watched Dai-Jeong walk in their direction. "It means 'I love you.'"

"Oh," said Cicely, and she smiled.

ACKNOWLEDGMENTS

*For Julie Andrews and Emma Walton:
their joyful vision brought this imprint to life,
and the book to print. For Katherine Tegen
and Julie Hittman, editors at HarperCollins,
for their suggestions and encouragement.*

*For my friends and family, especially Pamela
Holt, librarian and mentor, and Jeremiah
Creedon, writer and editor, with thanks for
all the advice and long-distance calls.*

*Love and gratitude immeasurable to Susie,
Lou Ann, and Charlotte for a hundred and
more Tuesday-night critiques (and Susie, the
pen was nowhere near thanks enough).*

*To my husband, Scott, and our sons, Per and
Ben: This story is my gift to you.*

And for tales, tellers, and children who listen.

Did you like this book? Julie Andrews would love to read your review of BLUE WOLF, or any of the books in the Julie Andrews Collection. Write to her at:

JULIE ANDREWS
THE JULIE ANDREWS COLLECTION
HarperCollins Children's Books, 1350 Avenue of the Americas
New York, NY 10019
or
info@julieandrewscollection.com

From time to time we will post reader reviews on the Julie Andrews Collection website. Please include permission to quote you, including your name and location, when you submit your review.

OTHER BOOKS YOU MIGHT ENJOY IN THE
JULIE ANDREWS COLLECTION:

DRAGON: *Hound of Honor*
by Julie Andrews Edwards and Emma Walton Hamilton

DUMPY AND THE FIREFIGHTERS
by Julie Andrews Edwards and Emma Walton Hamilton,
illustrated by Tony Walton

DUMPY TO THE RESCUE!
by Julie Andrews Edwards and Emma Walton Hamilton,
illustrated by Tony Walton

DUMPY'S APPLE SHOP
by Julie Andrews Edwards and Emma Walton Hamilton,
illustrated by Tony Walton

GRATEFUL: *A Song of Giving Thanks*
by John Bucchino, illustrated by Anna-Liisa Hakkarainen

THE LAST OF THE REALLY GREAT WHANGDOODLES
by Julie Andrews Edwards

THE LEGEND OF HOLLY CLAUS by Brittney Ryan

THE LITTLE GREY MEN
by BB, illustrated by Denys Watkins-Pitchford

MANDY by Julie Andrews Edwards

SIMEON'S GIFT
by Julie Andrews Edwards and Emma Walton Hamilton,
illustrated by Gennady Spirin